The concept behind *Winesburg, Indiana* seems almost impossible
to pull off: asking an all-star roster of small and major press writers
to contribute work to a fabulist linked story collection. . . . The
collection makes the argument that Indiana—not to mention
the greater Midwest—is more than just flyover country.

SALVATORE PANE, author of *Last Call in the City of Bridges*

This book is funny as hell, and beneath its humor are contemporary
grotesques who deepen our understanding of the human
condition, making us look unflinchingly at the darker side
of human nature and human loneliness, that universally felt
alienation common to isolated, repressed Midwestern towns and
therefore to almost any small town anywhere in the world.

LEX WILLIFORD, author of *Macauley's Thumb*

"Virginal" reconstructions, alien scat collectors, manchildren,
and toenail-eating reverends. *Winesburg, Indiana* reads like
a lung—it expands and holds the big emotions of its many
lives; each exhale is an inhabitant, inhabiting. It exists. It will
continue to exist, cease and desist demand be damned.

ZACH TYLER VICKERS, author of
Congratulations on Your Martyrdom!

You may be able to fly over Winesburg, Indiana, but more challenged to take it at ground level, where the Fork River cuts like a knife through the flat terrain. You may find that Winesburg, once discovered, is not easy to leave. A host of characters give voice to their wildest dreams, their dreariest defeats, their sweetest triumphs. The voices of forty denizens hold you in their home town, page after page.

JAN MAHER, author of *Heaven, Indiana*

Winesburg, Indiana may, or may not, speak with a forked tongue, or, at least, a tongue planted firmly in a cheek, but this compelling compendium also accomplishes the necessary task of surprising readers with an alternate Indiana. Here you will find forty of Indiana's most articulate observers and writers full of sass and humor as they take on a host of contemporary stereotypes, spinning them on their heads and leaving any reader dizzy with admiration.

WILLIAM O'ROURKE, author of *Confessions of a Guilty Freelancer*

Michael Martone, Bryan Furness, and their team of cartographers have taken their pens and knives to the town of Winesburg, Indiana to map out the varieties of human experience lived on the Fork River. They have succeeded in drawing a new prime meridian by which we may chart our joys and sorrows in these short fictions—plotting the intersections of trains and post office murals, cats and young lovers, faith healers and former high school football stars—finally discovering our own selves counted among the townspeople.

COLIN RAFFERTY, author of *Hallow This Ground*

WINESBURG, INDIANA

break away books

INDIANA UNIVERSITY PRESS

Bloomington & Indianapolis

WINESBURG, INDIANA

A FORK RIVER ANTHOLOGY

Edited by Michael Martone
and Bryan Furuness

This book is a publication of

INDIANA UNIVERSITY PRESS
Office of Scholarly Publishing
Herman B Wells Library 350
1320 East 10th Street
Bloomington, Indiana 47405 USA

iupress.indiana.edu

The paper used in this publication meets the
minimum requirements of the American
National Standard for Information
Sciences – Permanence
of Paper for Printed Library
Materials, ANSI Z39.48-1992.

Manufactured in the
United States of America

Library of Congress
Cataloging-in-Publication Data

Winesburg, Indiana : Fork River
anthology / edited by Michael
Martone and Bryan Furuness.
    pages cm. – (Break away books)
    Includes bibliographical
references and index.
    ISBN 978-0-253-01688-1 (pbk. :
alk. paper) – ISBN 978-0-253-01734-5
(ebook) 1. American literature – Indiana.
2. Indiana – Literary collections.
I. Martone, Michael, editor.
II. Furuness, Bryan, editor.
    PS571.16W56 2015
    810.8'09772 – dc23

                            2015013901

1 2 3 4 5   20 19 18 17 16 15

FOR
PATTY AND TONY MARTONE
MOTHER AND DAD
&
SUE AND DREW FURUNESS
MOM AND DAD

Contents

WINESBURG, INDIANA

CEASE AND DESIST DEMAND
Pursuant to Title 17 of the United States Code

City Manager
13 Spalding Street
Winesburg, Indiana 46712

Dear Sir or Madam:

This law firm represents the Town of Winesburg (Ohio). If you are represented by legal counsel, please direct this letter to your attorney immediately and have your attorney notify us of such representation.

It has been brought to our attention that your town, Winesburg (Indiana), has been using the Winesburg trademark in association with the marketing or sale of your products and services, namely, those of meditative introspection, synthetic emotional effects, general literary malaise, and cathartic artistic performances including but not limited to confessions, covetings, secrets-keeping, and the wholesale packaging and propagation of spent signature tears. It is possible that you were unaware of this conflict, so we believe that it is in our mutual interest to bring this matter to your attention.

Winesburg is a registered trademark of our municipality, Winesburg (Ohio), and is used in conjunction with the distribution of dramatic monologues and third-person narrations to invoke the grotesque and map the psychophysiological and neurotic manifestations of its inhabitants in order to derive empathic and epiphanic pleasure and/or pain in a controlled hermetic setting. Winesburg's federal trademark registration has been in full effect for over ninety (90) years, since shortly after the publication of the book of short stories *Winesburg, Ohio,* by Mr. Sherwood Anderson. That Winesburg, Ohio, refers to a fictional town of Mr. Anderson's own imagination, modeled on the town of Clyde, Ohio, whose malicious libel litigation with the estate of Mr. Anderson continues to this day. The trademarked village of Winesburg (Ohio) was constructed in 1920 in southwestern Paint Township of Holt County by Austrian Mesmerists fleeing the dissolution of the Austro-Hungarian Empire, aficionados of the book *Winesburg, Ohio,* and early practitioners and adherents of applied phrenology and Gestalt therapies. A copy of the federal trademark registration is attached for your reference as Exhibit A.

Our federal registration of this trademark provides us with certain proprietary rights. This includes the right to restrict the use of the trademark, or a confusingly similar trademark, in association with confusingly similar products or services such as the distribution of Sadness, Fear, Longing, and Confusion itself. We have patented Madness. We own Trembling. We extensively market Grief. We facilitate the Recovery of Emotionally Paralyzing Memories and the Reliving of Childhood Trauma. We distribute Dirges and provide for all manner of Despairing Confession and Ecstatic Revelation in this aesthetically framed and fictive community situated on a glacial declivity near the second-largest Amish settlement in the United States. The Lanham Act (the U.S. Trademark Act) also provides numerous remedies for trademark infringement and dilution, including but not limited to preliminary and permanent injunctive relief, money damages, a defendant's profits, provisions for the destruction or confiscation of infringing products and promotional materials, and, where intentional infringement is shown (as would be the case here), attorneys' fees and possible treble money damages.

It is urgent that we exercise our right to protect our trademark. It serves as an important and distinctive representation of the origin of our products. State and federal law supports our position that confusingly similar trademarks may cause confusion among customers. This confusion may cause substantial harm to the trademark by facilitating the loss of its effectiveness in establishing a distinct association between it, our products and services, and the town's goodwill.

Due to these concerns, and because unauthorized use of our federally registered trademark amounts to an infringement of our trademark rights, we respectively request that you cease and desist from any further use of the Winesburg trademark in association with the sale, marketing, distribution, promotion, or other identification of your products or services.

This letter is sent without prejudice to Winesburg (Ohio)'s rights and claims, all of which are expressly reserved. In addition to this certified mail, return receipt requested version, I am also sending you a copy of this letter by regular first-class mail in case you refuse to accept the certified mail version of this letter.

Please respond by letter, indicating your intention to cease and desist from the use of the Winesburg trademark, or any confusingly similar trademark, within ten (10) calendar days.

We hope that this issue may be resolved this way so we can avoid any further legal remedies as provided by state law and under federal law pursuant to the Lanham Act.

Sincerely,

Avery Nuit, Esq.

City Manager

The town of Winesburg operates under the weak-mayor system, always has. I am the city manager, a creature of the council charged by the council, five elected members, to keep the trash trucks running on time. There aren't too many other municipal services to attend to. The fire department is volunteer. The county provides the police. There are the sewers of the town, and I maintain them myself and conduct the daily public tours. The sewers of Winesburg are vast, channeling one branch of the Fork River through underground chambers and pools roofed with vaulted ceilings tiled with ceramic-faced bricks. The sewers were the last public works project of the Wabash and Erie Canal before the canal bankrupted the state of Indiana. I mentioned tours but there aren't that many tourists interested in sewers. I walk the tunnels alone, my footsteps on the paving stones echoing. The drip, drip, drip of the seeping water. The rapid splashing over the riprap. There is the landfill as well to manage, the heart-shaped hole where the fossil-rife limestone of the sewers was quarried, punched in the table-flat topography of a field north of Winesburg. We are located on the drained sandy bed of an ancient inland sea. Sea birds from the Great Lakes find their way to the pit, circle and dive down below the rim, emerging with beaks stuffed with human hair, for their nests, I guess. Indiana has complicated laws concerning the disposal of cut hair. Much of the state transships its hair here. A thriving cottage industry persists, that of locket making, using the spent anonymous hair to simulate the locks of a departed loved one. The lockets are afterthoughts, fictional keepsakes. The locket makers can be seen rummaging through the rubbish of the dump, collecting bags of damp felt. Winesburg was the first city in the country to install the emergency 911 telephone number. J. Edward Roush, member of the House of Representatives, was our congressman and was instrumental in establishing the system. I manage that too, taking a shift, at night usually, in the old switching room, to answer the calls of the citizens of Winesburg who more often than not do have something emerging. Usually not an acute emergency but more a chronic unrest. An anxiousness. Not a heart attack but a heartache. I listen. The switches, responding to the impulse of someone somewhere dialing, tsk and sigh and click. I manage. I am the city manager.

❋ ❋ ❋

I am not sure what to do with the cease and desist order I duly received from the town of Winesburg, Ohio. I am not sure I understand how to cease and desist the steeping municipal sadness here. It is not as if I or anyone here can help it. Years ago, Fort Wayne, the state's second-largest city twenty miles to the east, decided to exhume its dead and to become, like San Francisco, free of cemeteries and graveyards. The consequence of the decision meant transporting remains to multiple necropoli on the outskirts of Winesburg. The newly dead still arrive daily, carried by a special midnight-blue fleet of North American Van Lines tractor-trailers, escorted up the Lincoln Highway by the Allen County Sheriff's Department. I must admit, it is our biggest industry, bigger than the box factory, the eraser works, and the cheese product plant. We tend. We tend the dead. And the funereal permeates this place in the way fluoxetine, in all its manifestations, saturates the sewers of Winesburg, the spilled and pissed SSRIs of the citizenry sluicing into the water table beneath the fossil seabed of an ancient extinct inland sea. Our deathly still suburbs. Our industrious dust. Our subterranean chemistry. Our tenuous analog telephony. Our thin threads of wistful connection. What am I to do? How am I to cease, desist? Manage?

Amanda Patch

It all started innocently enough when I petitioned the Most Reverend Leo, bishop of the Diocese of Fort Wayne–South Bend, to initiate the beatification of Father Herman Heilmann, founder of the monastery, Our Lady of the Circumcision, here in Winesburg. Father Herman made a home for his brother fathers, who come from all over the country to this quiet cloistered retreat—a collection of cabins initially converted from the rundown Rail Splitter Motor Court off the old Lincoln Highway—to study and pray and meditate on that old Old Testament story of Abraham having to sacrifice his son Isaac to establish the covenant with the Lord. I just thought the Father's work needed to be recognized, so in addition to my letter-writing campaign, I convinced my reading group to concentrate on one book for a year, deeply meditating on the martyrs, spending each meeting discussing a life of a saint we read in Butler's *Lives of the Saints.* It was difficult, to say the least. The litanies of the deaths and the dying, the various methods of torture and the infliction of pain, seemed organized in such a way as to demonstrate the excruciating genius of Satan, working through his minions on earth, to exact utter and endless agony. My reading group, made up of several of the neighborhood's ladies and ladies from the church, also met on Wednesdays each spring to follow the March Madness of the basketball tournament, suspending our usual stock club meetings to substitute the brackets for the fine print of the big board. We were, perhaps, predisposed to such communal excitement, some might even say hysteria. As we read and reported on the lives of the saints, our presentations became more elaborate, the distinction between the mere abstract recounting of the material and actually living the lives of the *Lives of the Saints* became confused for us, and very soon we became enamored by the very particular narratives of the sainted virgins. We were impressed with the passion of their passion to remain undeflowered, intact, innocent, and dedicated to Jesus to the point of taking Our Savior as a wedded yet chaste husband. There were (I remember, how could I forget) multiple incinerations at the stake, crucifixions, beheadings, stonings, rapes, and sodomies with a variety of implements and animals in an effort to pry from these devoted young women the most special jewel in their possession. It was all quite thrilling. We were moved. The antique prose of the text added a musty patina of gothic authenticity to the recitations of anguish, courage, and ecstatic exultation. All of us, by this time, were far from our own corporeal purity, having given birth to nearly four dozen children among us. Many of us now were grandmothers as well. We had long suffered both the pangs of birthing and the fandangos of sexual intercourse, procreative and not, at the hands of our husbands and, dare I say, lovers. I am not sure whose idea it was initially, as many of us have used the skilled services of Dr. Minnick for other plastic operative rearrangements, but we somehow reached a consensus that all of us would participate in a kind of tontine in reverse. We would not so much wait to unstop the cork of a pilfered "liberated" brandy but to stop it all back up again in the first place. You have heard of women's clubs, such as ours, creating calendars of their members photographed tastefully nude, a fundraiser for charity. Our idea was only, we thought, a slight variation on such projects. Perhaps it was Dr. Minnick himself who suggested it, inviting us to consider reconstructive surgeries "down there," commenting that labia reduction was now his most performed and profitable operation, the norming and neatening up, if you will, of the pudenda to the standard folds and tufts, bolsters and grooves, of the ideal cosmetic model. Again, we were thrilled, that such miracles could be performed relatively painlessly in an outpatient setting. But I did know for a fact that this would not suit us. We proposed to Dr. Minnick that he attempt to go beyond the mere landscaping of what could be seen but also seek the unseen, to take us back in time. To state it simply—to reattach our long-gone maidenhoods, cinching closed once more the orifice of our experience, virginal once more. And this he did, was anxious to do. Inventing a kind of embroidered helmet for the task, he wove the cap together from multicolored and multigauged sutures, a kind of monofilament cartilage tissue. The truth is when we are together now, reading further into the lives of the saints and the endless mortifications of the flesh, we continue to admire, in great detail, during our break for cookies and tea, his handiwork performed on each and every one of us, and how such emendations have delivered us all, strangely beautiful and pristine, one step closer to God.

Cleaning Lady to the Stars

Call me Isobelle—at least, that's what my card says. I'd like it better if you call me the cleaning lady to the stars, a.k.a. the professors at St. Meinhof's. They move in here trailing a van full of kitchen gear they don't know how to use, wearing their attitudes like tiaras. One of them got the card made up for me 'cause she thought it was cute. I thought it was embarrassing, but she was right about one thing: you got to have a business card if you want to scrub professors' toilets. They check references, too.

"How you like the Midwest?" I ask the new customers, first time I show up with a mop.

"You mean the Mid*waste*?" They ask me where you go to *eat* around here. You go to your well-stocked kitchen, is what I'm thinking, but I point them to Albert's Seafood Lounge, and it's not entirely my fault if they swallow a little botulism with their sushi. We didn't have sushi till Albert thought to bring it in and (in case you hadn't noticed how far we are from the ocean) we survived without it.

The land that time forgot, the professors call Winesburg. They say they'll probably only be here a couple of years, 'cause they're really East Coast people or West Coast people, or if they're truly obnoxious, Texas people. Twenty years later, here is where they're still parked, with their tenure and their season football tickets, and the same forty pounds the rest of us put on since high school. Meanwhile their paychecks have been getting fatter, too, not that they ever do any work *I* can see, and they've moved on out to the subdivisions with the fruity-tooty gazebos and the house-moats just in case a marauding army's passing by. I haven't noticed no raise in *my* hourly.

All right, I say to myself. All right, let me play me some Taylor Swift nice and loud as a consolation: nothing like a little young blood to perk up your spirits while you're brushing the high-paid shit off her highness's throne. But if somebody's doing her *"research"* at home, I'm not allowed even that consolation. "Oh, Izzy, just a *smidge* lower. Well, maybe a little lower than *that.*"

You find all *kinds* of things slipped behind their beds and it's another consolation that we're all the same under the skin, only you know they're paying way too much for a vibrating riding crop to arrive in a plain unmarked package when Doug could get one at Boys Will Be Boys out by the bypass for half the price. But this new customer downtown in the miserable Victorian with the sagging floors is more Girls Will Be Boys, anyway. Her name's Betty, old-fashioned and plain like you'd never expect with her purple-tipped spikes. She's as buff as the boys' wrestling coach and she spends *a whole lot of time* on Craigslist, if you catch my drift.

She's in English where they put all the troublemakers, I've learned over the years—so good, she's feisty, let's ask her to Trivia Night. My pardner Lucille and me been begging professors to go to Trivia Night at St. Casimir's for as long as we've been cleaning, 'cause that's the scam around here: you get you some PhDs and you've got you a winning trivia team. Not that they could do it without us. Lucille and me got to cover TV shows, sports teams, astrology, politics, radiology, and quantum mechanics. But you can count on pretty much any professor, no matter what they claim to teach, for geography, cooking (naturally), gardening, the Kinks, and foreign languages. When they're doing accents it's embarrassing to even be sitting at the same table with them.

Betty says sure, she'll give the St. Caz Trivia Night a whirl. I suggest the Polish supper first, but as soon as Lucille and me are salivating over the brats, Betty laughs: she only does *raw* food anymore. So *that* explains those torture machines taking up all the counter space in her kitchen. Something sweet about her tattoos—she's got one pumping heart on her right bicep that says *Dewey Dell 4-Evuh*—makes me do what I've never done before and tell her just come on over to the house and we'll eat there first.

"Why thank you, ma'am," she says, and am I imagining or is that a Sarah Palin–size wink she gives me? I'll kill her if she's making fun. Lucille digs me in the ribs on the way out to the truck. "What *you* gonna make that's *raw*?"

"Albert's sushi!" We both get the giggles till we pee our pants. I'm thinking, anybody can make coleslaw and put out a bowl of walnuts, which is exactly what I do come Saturday night. Betty says, "Perfect, my favorite meal"—I sure to hell hope she's not making fun of me—and then she holds up the bottle of wine she's brought. Probably she sees the looks on our faces 'cause now she hoists a corkscrew, like she thought I wouldn't *have* one. "It's not that," I say, meaning I prefer a no-fuss-no-muss American beer to a mediocre Pinot Noir like the one she brought, but Lucille beats me to the sarcasm punch: "We'd rather smoke a little crank before Trivia."

Betty's eyes get as fiery as that pumping heart on her big arm and she says, "You mean crystal *meth*?" Poor baby. Once they're in Winesburg hobnobbing with the help, these professors think they're in white-trash hell. I get her a Miller and I'm sorry to disappoint her. But she's already sniffing around the living room like an overstimulated terrier and hits a few keys on the electric piano, where Doug has his little statuette of Liszt. Look, I *know* he's sentimental. It's not my statuette.

"You play?" Betty asks me, and I say, "Only honky-tonk," God's own truth. So she moves on to read the walls, plastered with clippings from the All-American Girls Professional Baseball League. My great-aunt Tommie played third base for the Fort Wayne Daisies.

"Wow," Betty says, "you're a real *scholar* of this baseball stuff, aren't you?"

"Hell, you should see her Billy Sunday room," Lucille says, and I give her the evil eye. I don't want any professors in my Billy Sunday room, but you can guess what happens next, now that all the walnuts are gone. Nothing to do but show her and make her take her shoes off first. That is *white* shag and I mean to keep it that way. Betty's a good sport—takes off her socks too—and digs her toes in. She doesn't even fuss when I take her beer away, 'cause Billy, bless his heart, was a Prohibitionist. Betty studies the pictures like she's a scholar, too—I've got them divided into baseball on one wall and hellfire on the next. On the paneling, there's a row of Billy preaching and playing together. She says, "How'd a Catholic get interested in an evangelist?"

She thinks I'm a Catholic 'cause of trivia night at St. Caz but I'd rather not discuss my lack of religious affiliation with an employee of St. Meinhof's, which pretty much *owns* Winesburg, so I just laugh. Lucille thinks she's helping when she says, "Isobelle has long talks with Billy."

14

"Lu*cille*."

Too late. Betty gets it out of me that I've been known to hold a séance or two and Billy Sunday has been known to make an appearance. I never would have let it get this far if she hadn't dug her toes into my carpet so pretty or given me that wink.

Now she gets all tooled up. How's my séance work? Do I turn the lights off? (Lucille's just turned them off for me.) Do I call his name? (Duh.) Do I have a Ouija board or some such? When I say, no, I call him on my iPhone, she lets out a roar of laughter and that does it: Billy's got to get in the game and stand up for me.

"Are you mocking this good lady, Professor?" he says—not in his hellfire voice, in his gentle-Jesus voice, like he's sorely disappointed. He's wearing his old White Stockings uniform, which is falling off him, he lost so much muscle before he passed. I suppose he might not even know he comes back as a little old man.

"No, sir," says Betty, her voice a-trembling, beads of sweat dancing on her upper lip, where she has the lightest little mustache. It's kind of fetching.

Bill revs up to hit her with *Have you been saved, Professor,* which could be downright embarrassing to all of us, so I get him chatting instead about the Winesburg Wildcats. His Christianity doesn't stop him from being nasty on *that* subject. Lucille has meanwhile helped Betty sit on the couch, but she looks like she's about to topple off that and hit the floor, she's so scared.

"Don't you worry," I say. "It's just Billy Sunday. He's got a lake house not that far from here."

Her lips are turning blue and I don't know how to tell Billy it's time for him to make himself scarce. He's so sensitive in his old age. Betty commences to mutter and we all lean forward to hear her:

"All this *religion.*"

Billy gets his stern look on but Betty's trash-talking religion must have hurt him bad 'cause he's fading too. "Wait," I call, maybe to both of them, thinking I can bring them together after all, but before we know it Lucille and me are sitting in the dark with a passed-out Betty and Billy Sunday departed back to Winona Lake. My iPhone buzzes to beat the band—probably Douglas is texting me. *Go away,* I hiss to the phone, but Betty hears in her sleep and sits halfway up like she's seen a ghost.

"I'll go," she says, into the darkness, and Lucille and me say, "No! No, we need you on our trivia team. The pot's up to almost seven hundred bucks." Betty says she knew she shouldn't have come here, but I know she doesn't mean my house, she means Winesburg.

"Aw, don't be all stuffy," I tell her. "We might surprise you."

And we help her to her feet and get her out the room till she's looking more like her feisty self. Safe back in the kitchen, I do mention that a living wage and a little time off would be appreciated, and I admit I do it in a kind of spooky-séancy-Midwestern way, but she perks right up at that and says, "Isobelle, I used to be the graduate student *union rep,*" and then she gives me another of those winks—talk about spooky, she's Sarah Palin *exactly*—and I know we're going to win that trivia pot together. We all three go marching out of my house with our arms linked, singing "Solidarity Forever," and Betty allows that she really wasn't expecting any Field of Dreams crap in my little house.

I'm hurt the way Bill was hurt, but I'm used to it. Professors. No social skills whatsoever, which is why they ended up doing what they do.

Jackie Patch

My mother's way is not my way. You must find your own way. There are many ways. Those who claim to know the way, the One Way, are speaking only for themselves, and are trying to get a volume discount in God's supermarket of grace and life everlasting. I know this because Reverend Dave told me. It was he who opened my eyes, unstoppered my ears, clipped my toenails, and defibrillated my heart. I left the church, but I never stopped believing in God, or something like God—a Prime Mover, a Great Spirit, a Shake-and-Baker, a Mixmaster, a Lotte Lenya. My mother raised me Catholic, then I became Episcopal, then Unitarian, then a pantheist, then a Hare Krishna (I didn't like the robes or the haircuts), then born again, then Rastafarian, then nothing—a spiritual agnostic, I suppose—before settling on a nondenominational church run by a Reverend Dave and two lesbian former nuns who are raising their sons (Reverend Dave donated his Essence to both of them so they could each have children) in a deconsecrated church on Wentworth Avenue that they have turned into the First Family of Christ Living Center and Day Care. My spiritual journey took me about twenty years. I knew I was looking for something, and in this community I have found it. Caring for Stephen and Jacob and the other children entrusted to us is a calling from a Higher

Power. This I believe. Grace fills you up from the bottom of your feet right up past your eyeballs until it pours out of your ears like wax after you've stoppered your ears up with warm water to let the wax soften. You feel purified and rare and not at all forsaken, which is what I felt when my mother first got involved in that prayer group. My mother wanted my sister and me (I pray for Julie's soul, she is a lost sheep, a wayward soul, and two-thirds of the way toward being a Godless infidel) to hew to the religion in which we were baptized, but I couldn't do that. Instead I found Reverend Dave and the First Family of Christ Living Center and Day Care. And Reverend Dave has found me. Reverend Dave took me when I was at my lowest and Lo! he raised me up on high. He cares for me, body and soul. "Christ washed the feet of his apostles, did you know that?" he asked me, and so he washed my feet, stroking the curves of my ankles, touching his tongue to my instep—"a holy place," he told me—and observing that my toenails, while blessed with luscious half-moons ("the lips of God have touched you here," he said), needed trimming. "We are a vessel of the Lord's making," he told me, clip-clipping, "and nothing that is of us should go to waste," which is why he saved the toenail clippings to sprinkle on his peanut butter and pickle sandwiches—trimmings as trimming. As he masticated he told me, "Ingesting that which is removed from the body's temple is a symbolic manifestation of the circle of life. Did you know that the only living part of your toenail is called the matrix? It is underneath the nail fold, which overlaps the nail itself, and it is in the matrix where the keratin, which forms the nail you see, is created. The lunula—those moons you see—are the shadow of the matrix. You understand now, don't you? Your feet, your lovely, holy feet, contain the Shadow of the Matrix. Keratin, related to Kristos, Greek for Messiah, the Christ, is a feast for one's soul. Henceforth, whenever I trim your toenails, it shall be a feast day." Reverend Dave is a believer in feast days. He is a believer in the body as a temple. He believes—as I believe, for he has told me—that entering the temple is a great and holy thing. This, too, is part of the circle of life. He removes the keratin from my toes, he ingests the keratin in his sandwiches, and this keratin, in turn, becomes part of his Essence, which he must give back to my temple. "There are many ways in which the body is a temple," he says, "just as the Shadow of the Matrix manifest in your toes is but a Shadow of the Matrix that is in you, and I, Reverend Dave, must make deposits in the Shadow of the Matrix to keep holy your temple." He showed me how this was done, and Lo! that night he speared my soul, raising me up high and lowering me, over and over, saying, "Rise up and lower yourself for His Humble Servant, the Reverend Dave, and I will make my deposit in your temple, and thus will the Matrix of Life be entwined, thee and me, and Oh, Jackie, Oh, it shall be good, yes, yes, yes, it shall be good." And the Reverend Dave showed me that there are many ways into the temple, and in the morning left me broken and bleeding and in love with him, for all that he had done for me, and he told me that my toenail trimmings had filled him with an excess of Essence, which he needed to give back to my Matrix, so the circle of life could be complete, and we feasted like that for many days and nights, until I felt queasy in the mornings, and the Shadow of my Matrix began to balloon and swell, and then Reverend Dave told me that there are, in fact, many temples, and he was worried we would not be able to sustain the circle of life with just my toenail clippings feeding his Essence, and so he introduced me to new temples that he had found, Karla and Alison and Susan and Melissa and Amy and Rachel and Monica and Samantha and Jessica and Debra and Ann, and he told us all that he was grateful he had found us, repositories of the Matrix which generated the toenails which fed his Essence which he could deposit back into us, his dozen disciples, his dozen temples, oh happy day when these many ways into the Matrix were made known to him and could receive his Essence, for he was certain that in this way the First Family of Christ Living Center and Day Care would grow and expand just as our temples would grow and expand until we pushed new beings out into the world, little miracles that were a combination of our Matrixes and his Essence, and in this way we would be blessed with local, state, and federal funds as a charter school and day care facility. The only problem, it seemed to me, was that as the Shadow of our Matrix began to balloon and swell, Reverend Dave would stop giving us his Essence, and instead concentrate his efforts only on those temples who had not yet commingled his Essence with our Matrix to the point where such a commingling was visible. It seemed to me he stopped worshipping our feet as well, and those of us with a swelling Matrix grew toenails long and yellow, and even though Reverend Dave assured us he was simply waiting for the blessed expelling of the miracle from each of us, and letting us restore ourselves, whereupon he would again worship at our feet and clip our nails and give us his Essence, making us, he said, the Matrix Reloaded, we began—I began, at least—to doubt the sincerity of his intentions. But Reverend Dave reassured us, No, no, he treasured us all, equally, it was just that his Essence was required elsewhere, and he instructed us each to be the keepers of our temples, to trim our nails ourselves, and keep these Shavings of Keratin in jars labeled with our names, and when it was time for him to gift us again with his Essence he would have the necessary trimmings to begin again, anew, each of us clear, fresh vessels for his seed. But of course as we grew great with miracles we could no longer bend over to trim and collect our keratin ourselves. This was an ablution the two ex-nuns performed for us, and we for each other, our Matrixes (Matri?) swollen and hard as watermelons, and in the absence of Reverend Dave we explored the contours of our feet ourselves. We explored other things as well. We did this as a group, though we paired up for the explorations. Monica, who was the first (after me) to have successfully received the Reverend Dave's Essence said, "You know what? Reverend Dave is right. There are many ways in which the body is a temple, and there are many ways into the temple," and with her fingers she showed me some, and I trembled with understanding. And after many nights of exploration we agreed, as a group, that when it was time again for Reverend Dave to again grace us with his Essence perhaps we would not be the willing receptacles he thought we should be. Perhaps we would tell him to take a hike.

Julie Patch

My mother is effing nuts. I would like to put this more politely, to be sure: she is touched, she is suffering pre-dementia, she has her spells, she was never the sharpest tool in the shed, and over time she's gotten duller, she is rationality-challenged, her marbles are not all where she first found them, she's not quite right in the head, her screws are not as tight as they could be, she's gone around the bend a bit, she's not on her rocker, the light in her attic has dimmed, there are bats in her belfry, etc. But the fact is she's gone absolutely bonkers. She's nutty as a fruitcake. She's stark raving mad. She's batty, loony, bananas, cuckoo, crazy, dotty, screwy, schizo, psycho, mad as a hatter. She has taken leave of her senses, cracked up, gone wacko, she's unhinged, disturbed, psychotic, deranged, demented, she's certifiable, she's crazy, a lunatic, non compos mentis, mad as a March hare. In short, she is a total nutjob. My sister Jackie, too. My sister Jackie in spades. Mind you, it is not my mother or my sister's religious devotion that causes me to say this. I think spirituality is a very important part of one's life. But this is not about spirituality. This is about carnal pleasure and displeasure masquerading as holiness. It's sick, all of it. Rebuilding your hymen? Turning the clock back on your virginity? Coming up with some elaborate word game about your Matrix and your Essence so you don't have to admit you got laid by Reverend Dave? WTF, as they say in the text messages. I'd be ROFLing if it weren't so sad, so pathetic. I mean, my life is no carpet of carnations—a five-year-old kid and a thirty-one-year-old ex-husband who's going on seventeen as far as I can tell, and a dead-end job at the DMV followed by two nights a week cocktail waitressing at the Fort Wayne Holiday Inn out on Nine Mile Road by the airport, where the businessmen think the outfit they make you wear (black tights and a black miniskirt and a ruffled white blouse unbuttoned down to there) gives them carte blanche to stare down your shirt front and pinch your thighs as you walk by—but the bottom line is I suck it up and get on with it. I have defense mechanisms. I have a sense of self. Somebody's hand grazes my behind and I tell them they try that again I'll break every finger they own. It hurts my tips except for the ones who actually like the abuse because it means somebody's paying attention. But I have my pride. I'm not going to lie down for anybody, like my sister did, and I'm not going to celebrate a self-enforced sexlessness while I read about flagellations and stonings and dismemberments and other acts of violence that get transfigured into religious porn for those scared of their own desire. You have a body, people, own it! To be honest, though, not that I did a whole lot better at first. I mean, in college I drank a lot and went home with a lot of losers. I fell in love with one of them (that would be you, Leo), and compounded my error by marrying him. Turned out he wanted the same thing they all wanted, didn't much want me after he got it, only by then we were already mediocrely wed. Particulars aside, in other words, I wasn't much different from my sister Jackie, who clutches her hands over her belly and tells me Reverend Dave worships her temple or her Matrix or whatever word he's using these days to get inside her drawers. But Violet was a gift, however poor the source (I'm talking about you, Leo), and that's something. I just wish her father shared that belief, that children are a gift, and you must provide for them. Leo doesn't have a protective bone in his body—unless you're talking about his gift for self-preservation. For cutting and running. For skating on his responsibilities. He works first shift at the tool and die plant (when it's running)—he's a floor manager because he's got a degree—and he could help with the child care sometimes, but no, that would cut into his drinking time after work. Mom's too wrapped up in her *Lives of the Saints* to take much of an interest in the life of her granddaughter, and Jackie says I could drop her off at the First Family of Christ Living Center and Day Care, but I'd be worried Reverend Dave would take an interest in my daughter's ankles. Or her toenails. So instead of having my family step up I'm hiring sitters the evenings I'm slinging drinks. And I'm still going home with the wrong sort of men. Sometimes you do get lonesome for the company. Once I even called Leo. "I knew you'd come around," he said, shucking his jeans while we were still having a glass of wine on the sofa, and that's when I threw him out for the second time in my life. I realized I wasn't that desperate. But there's something in me, something like a weakness, that makes me desperate anyway. Every few weeks or so I find myself doing the walk of shame at 2 AM from some two-bit apartment complex across the parking lot to my car and paying the sitter twice what I should because they had to stay three hours later than I said I needed them. That or some guy is telling me as he's zipping himself, "I'll call you," and he never calls, and I know he's not going to call, but as he's gently pulling the door closed behind him with happiness and relief and I'm lying there all scummy-mouthed and broken-hoped but semi-in-love-with this guy who just used me, I'm still believing he might be the one, or I'm telling myself he's the last one like that before I meet the one, the really-for-real one, perhaps the very next night, I tell myself, I just have to open my legs and hope—

Tell me, is that so different from my sewed-up mother or my knocked-up-by-her-minister-with-the-foot-fetish sister? I must be effing nuts.

Dale Rumsey

It's the wife's family business. We have the concession, pumping the latrines, outhouses, comfort stations, porta-potties, and septic tanks over at the big Henry David Thoreau County Park. The park's in the floodplain and sprawls along the river's swampy, scrubby, piney bottomland—many acres where the sun don't shine. It is a known fact that most of the alien abductions take place here. Or so it seems. It makes sense this is the place where the aliens come to abduct folks. The park is remote and rural with many secluded nooks and crannies and hidden glens surrounded by stands of virgin forest. There is a high percentage of Winesburgians who have reported their live vivisections, endoscopies, anal probes, and invasive explorations. Folks disappear from these woods every day, the fires in the grills still smoldering, only to appear, days later, naked as God made them, staggering through the stands of quaking aspen, swaying birch, and seeding cottonwood. They're a mess. And in my role as custodian, I have started a collection of alien scat left behind on these occasions, I suspect, when the spaceships jump into hyperdrive or through the wormholes or whatever. The crews do a little light housekeeping, I gather, before they shove off. One day I will have enough such samples to open a museum. I assume the visitors from outer space use the facilities themselves before commencing with their deliberate cathartic probings on us humans. They wash their hands or flippers or tentacles after relieving themselves. The water hereabouts is potable, artesian. The pumping facilities are over near the ruins of the old windmill and water tank that looks, now that I think about it, like some space saucer itself. Back to the scat. The first thing that strikes you (after the wide range of consistencies) is the variety of colors that shade into the blues and violets or are marbled with veins of orange or fluorescent flecks of green, chunked with copper, gold, or silver. Some leavings, years later, still radiate heat that is generated from something more than your normal mechanisms of decomposition. One elongated turd came equipped with what I can only imagine is its own treatment system—alien protozoa that then ingest the crap and excrete their own manure, leaving trails of slime in a kind of woodland forest camouflage pattern impossible to detect unless you are looking for it. Other piles are left behind wrapped in a kind of otherworldly wrapping paper, a frozen ribbon of blood-red urine tying up the package in a neat bow that, over time, subliminally evaporates into rusty ropey smoke. Or the waste is encapsulated in a stonelike outer shell of coprolite, a kind of geode or chocolate bonbon with a gooey soft center. I suspect that like many travelers our visiting anthropologists experience irregularity sparked by their own unfamiliarity with the microbial life they have to ingest while on the road. The liquefied residue, in certain spots, can be prodigious, and often I've found that the semisolid piles seem to steam, outgassing helium instead of methane or, even more remarkably, neon, which, when it sees the light of day, becomes excited and illuminates itself into drifting clouds of flickering pastel colors. Many aliens seem to ruminate, and the expectorant is as colorful and interesting as the other excretions, and a number of the extraterrestrials also seem to be coprophagic, like rabbits, expelling, after partial digestion, edible pellets that are then consumed. I have found such pellets with what I only can guess are alien teeth marks left behind in haste, the toilet stumbled upon by an innocent lost terrestrial hiker. Needless to say, I have found this strange poop mixed in with the everyday earthen spoil, as the abductions often include bowel scoping and the local subject must also endure a pre-op purgative enema of the GI tract before the procedure is to begin. I also pump the holding tanks at the outpatient clinics in town where more pedestrian colonoscopies are performed. Heck, I have had that procedure myself, studied with interest the photography of my insides out. Not gutsy so much as I have a professional curiosity. What creeps me out about all this is not the fecal matter but the drugs that seem universally applied by aliens and gastroenterologists alike to wipe clean the memory of the event. When one is under, one is not so much under, but instead says anything and everything, a kind of logorrhea, to the occupied operating staff. Who knows, perhaps the spacemen are much more interested in what comes out of our mouths than our anuses. In my expert opinion no one's shit don't stink, even the alien kind. But I have gotten used to it. Still, I have never gotten used to this other odor. The stench of our own stories is so attractive to us—bug-eyed and antenna-twitching carrion-eating creatures that we are.

Limberlost

Here's what I tell myself: I'm a mime and this town is the invisible box that I only pretend to be stuck in. Its boundaries are wherever I press the flat of my hand. Look, I'm trapped! Look, now I trace a window with my burglar gloves and peek through. Now I lift the window, climb through, and escape. Now I'm juggling. Now I'm dancing. Now the invisible box disappears. It never existed. Ha ha ha.

Or: I'm a crow, one of the screeching thousands that perch on the bare tree branches along the river like quarter notes on a skewy treble clef, then fly away in melancholy chords. Just passing through.

I'm not even from here. I came from somewhere else, voluntarily. No one made me come. I just did. I came for the PhD. Lots of people get here that way, to get them or give them. We say we're just passing through, but we're all still here when the birds return the next year.

The high schools are named after a president, a saint, and a poet. My neighbor, whose sons attended the poet high school, named his dog after the high school. I don't think he knew that he'd named his dog after a poet. This is something you find funny when you're getting a PhD in the humanities. Until the neighbor's poet-pet, leashed to a tree even as the temperature sinks and sinks, barks and barks while you (I) try to write a dissertation. And every (woof!) other (woof!) word (woof!) is (woof!) woof. Then you (I) realize it was never funny to begin with.

I didn't get the PhD. I got pregnant.

Winters are hard here. Long, cold, snow. He was warm. He had an actual functioning fireplace in his apartment, and Merlot by the boxful. No dog woofing outside. Books all over his shelves, his kitchen table, his nightstand. And records! With sleeves and needles, A-sides and B-sides. How we talked and read and danced and drank and and and. Oh, the humanities.

That was over a decade ago. It's more like something I read about than something I did. A minor chapter in a long novel.

He was gone by the time the baby was ABD: All But Delivered. November arrived and so did my Mia. Spring semester began in the deep of winter, and I became an adjunct teacher in the department of Sure, I Can Teach That. On the first day of class my main goal was to select a babysitter from among my students, and to woo her. The problem was that I needed babysitters during class time, so I had to find multiple sitters. Fortunately, my main adjuncting gig was at the all-girls Catholic college, which is positively loaded with maternal instincts.

That's where I met Becky. She was not the first person you'd select to care for your infant daughter, and she was not the first person I selected. I chose Front-Row Rose. French-Braid Rose. Four-Point-o Rose.

Would Rose be willing to watch Mia while I taught my other classes? Oh, totally. Did she understand all of my instructions about heating the bottle in hot water? Yeah, totally. Did she think

Mia was the cutest baby ever? OMG, totally. Did I trust her? Totally.

Most of the students at the college, including Rose, are from Elsewhere. From good families and good pasts that seem to promise even better futures. Becky, on the other hand, is from here. "From here." That's how she said it when we finally spoke. Purple-Nailed Becky. Messenger-Bagged Becky. What's-In-Your-Head Becky.

She reminded me of Elnora Comstock from the Limberlost novel, set a hundred years ago but not too far away from here. It was one of many books from my own youth that I had arranged on a bookcase to read with Mia. We would read them together and travel to places like Limberlost and the Laura Ingalls Wilder home. Becky reminded me of Poor Elnora, who arrives at school with old clothes and no books and thinks, "It was all a mistake; this was no school, but a grand display of enormous ribbon bows." Ribbon-Bow Rose. I was projecting of course, but it made me sympathetic to Becky, curious.

When I got Becky's first paper I still hadn't heard her speak in class. What would she have to say? It turned out that she had to say exactly what she was told to say in exactly the way she was told to say it. And yet she revealed nothing at all. This was Composition. Put these two texts in conversation with one another. Make an argument about how they connect, how they diverge. It was brilliant, really, how she was able to satisfy the assignment, write more than a thousand words, and say nothing.

Soon it was time for student conferences. Winter had settled in, the long hard snow of it. A year earlier I'd lived in a world of music, Merlot, and maps for a dissertation. Now my life was Mia and

Composition. And Reliable Rose, whose conference took place at my kitchen table over cinnamon tea. Becky arrived at my office late for her first conference. Mia was nestled in her pumpkin seat at my feet, and each of my students oohed and aahed over her, asked about her age and sleeping habits, and stared at her through most of the conference. Except Becky, who hardly acknowledged her at all.

I didn't need to discuss Becky's paper, which would get an A. So I asked where she was from, hopeful to piece together some of her mystery.

"From here."

It took a moment to register her meaning. Maybe because it was the first I'd heard her voice. But suddenly something, everything, made sense. "Which high school did you go to?" I asked. "President, saint, or poet?"

She didn't miss a beat of what I thought was my own private joke. "President."

"Jefferson," I said. The worst of the schools. Yet somehow she'd learned to write perfectly meaningless A papers and get herself into this college.

I imagined the rest of the Limberlost details of her life: spurned by her own mother, unable to afford better clothes, eager for an education. This made me reach out to her, talk to her over coffee in the Student Union (where I learned details worse than Limberlost), and root for her. But it did not make me ask her to babysit.

Until the afternoon Rose had to cancel. Rose was a new member of the Student Government committee and they were hosting a campus event, a comedienne (and I only recall this now because the image of that woman on the poster with the date and time remains in my mind like the last bits of baby food that you can never quite scrape from the inside of the jar). Rose had to be at the event. She told me after our class together, and by that time Becky was the only other person in the room. My options were limited: I could either cancel class—a dicey proposition for someone whose contract expired at the end of every semester—or ask Becky to fill in. I liked Becky; I trusted Rose.

I looked at Becky. She looked at the floor.

We could both feel the request in the air, and the fact that I wasn't asking it was embarrassing us both. *Oh, for God's sake,* I told myself. *It's just a fill-in. It's just one time. Everything will be fine.* So I gave her my most assured smile and said, "So, do you want to make some extra money next week?"

✻　✻　✻

Becky arrived at my door wearing her usual oversized black sweatshirt and military messenger bag. Pins lined the strap that crossed her chest, and I thought of her as a decorated Girl Scout. You see what you want to see.

"Let me show you where everything is," I said, leading her to the table where my papers were piled up for grading, and where Mia was mounted on her bouncer seat like a Thanksgiving turkey. I started to say something about Mia's favorite toys, but Becky was looking at the wall. "What are these?" she asked.

On my walls were framed antique maps of faraway places that no longer existed. Places with new names and new borders, places I tried to write about in my dissertation.

"Those are Plan A," I said. "Funny, huh? I came *here* to become an expert in those places." I unbuckled Mia and picked her up.

"And this is Plan B, Plan Baby." I lifted her to my shoulder and pressed my lips to her ear. "Aren't you, Mia? Plan Baby Mia." I kissed her a hundred times, breathed in her baby scent. God, I hope I did that.

"Are you going to finish?" Becky asked. "Your degree?"

I consulted Mia. "Are we going to finish? We don't know, do we?"

"You should finish and leave," Becky said. "Or just leave. Get out of Dodge."

I rocked Mia, patting her back. Becky had told me bits about her home life, her brother's meth problem, her parents' fights about it.

Then she said, as if the idea had just come to her, or as if she wanted it to look that way: "And you could take me with you."

"What's that?"

She spoke in a sudden rush. "You could leave and take me with you. I could help with Mia. You could finish your degree."

Her tone was pleading, and her request was too intimate, of course, totally inappropriate and certainly disproportionate to our relationship, but it stirred me because it was something I'd wanted to hear. I gazed at the maps on my walls. It was what I had wanted Mia's father to say to me.

But my sleep-deprived mind was on more practical matters: the semester, the cost of diapers, the class I was about to teach.

"Right now I do have to leave," I said, "for class. I'm going to put Mia down for her nap. You ought to have an easy time; she should sleep until I get back. Won't you, Mia-Moo? Say hi to Becky." I held up Mia's arm and waved it.

"Hi, Mia. Bye, Mia," Becky said, a bit dejected, as I carried Mia to the room we shared.

It's too easy to think it wouldn't have happened if Rose had been there. But I do, I can't help myself. When I returned home after my classes, Becky—Blameless Becky, It's-Not-Your-Fault-But-I-Blame-You-Anyway Becky—was on the couch watching TV. Mia had been dead for at least an hour.

My Mia. Sweet Mia. Sudden-Infant-Death Mia.

Limberlost was named Loblolly Marsh until the night Limber Jim got lost and never came back. Limberlost is a real place, an enormous swamp preserved by the state. I've never been there, but I have memories of it from reading the book as a kid. Mia would be ten now, and we would be reading it together and planning those trips now. In my mind, though, we've already gone a thousand times. My memories are of a place I've never been and events that never happened. My mind is its own Limberlost—a swampland full of moths, dragonflies, and Indian relics. A place to search for treasure, to get lost, to drown.

I saw Becky the other day. What else could make me go on like this now?

Grocery-Basketed Becky. Highlighted-Hair Becky. Baby-Bjorn Becky. I instinctively hid my face and tried to hide from the moment. Was it her? Unmistakably. Would I reveal myself? Make her see me? Make her see me see her baby? Even if I wanted that, I wasn't sure I could do it. The grocery aisle became a swampland beneath my feet. I might sink into the ground, and would she notice? Would she stop it from happening?

I hadn't seen her since that day. Someone took over my classes for the rest of the semester, and Becky disappeared. Maybe she found a way out of this town. Maybe she returns every year to see her patchwork family. Or maybe she only came now because of the baby. Her baby.

"What's her name?" I said. I don't recall making the decision to reveal myself, but I was suddenly standing beside her, sinking really, as she surveyed rows of pasta sauce. The baby strapped to her had a pink hat.

"Hmm?" Becky looked distracted but prepared to tolerate a stranger's pleasantries. I remember so clearly. How the faces of strangers were never kinder than when Mia was with me.

But when Becky turned to me, her distracted expression transformed into something else, something as apt and empty as her compositions once were, as cryptic as the buttons on her messenger bag. I'm sure my own expression changed upon seeing her so close, these ten years later, the scent of a newborn between us.

Winter was once again settling into its deep chill. "Home for the holidays?" I said.

"Yes." She covered the baby's pink hat with her left hand. "I live out east. Boston area."

Not only did she have new hair, tasteful makeup, a new town, a baby—she had a wedding ring, a big one. Some do make it out of this town, apparently. Some do get their happy ending. Who would have thought it would be Becky? But at the end of the Limberlost novel, even Elnora Comstock marries the man she loves and finally gets her mother's love, her happy ending.

"You look well," I said.

She winced, as if her bounty hurt her more than it hurt me.

"You're still here," she said in a low voice. It came out a question, one that I felt compelled to answer. But neither of us wanted to hear about how I couldn't leave Mia, and how, even if I'd wanted to, I had nowhere to go.

So what could I tell her?

Here's what I finally knew: I'm a ghost. A woman who wandered into this swamp of a town, got lost, and never made it out.

So like a ghost, I disappeared from the store, leaving my half-filled cart in the aisle, leaving Becky there with her baby and her ring and her life.

But not before I looked into Becky's eyes and found an answer I could give her.

What I told her was this: "I'm from here now."

Raymond Snow

I was wearing mittens because the warehouse was cold as hell so maybe I didn't have as good a grip on the forklift's wheel as I thought I did when I slipped my blades into the skip, and somebody must have got the load off-center because when I lifted, the forks hadn't gone all the way in, and the TVs—the flat screens, plasmas break if you just fart in their general direction—sort of slouched on the pallet at about three feet up. So I sped up to try to force the fork all the way in. That's when I kinda tossed 'em into the shelving unit that tipped and hit another shelving unit that tipped too, but luckily there was a wall next, so it wasn't nearly as bad as it could have been.

Well, that's what they have insurance for.

Foreman, that was Wally, kept screaming words like stupid and drunk and shit like that but he got quiet when Mr. Hansen pulled up to the overhead door in that big turd-brown 1980s Cadillac because he—I mean Wally—was starting to remember that there was two joints smoked out in his car before the shift started and I'd only smoked one though I'd paid for two, though he did let me have a couple of chugs from the bottle of Beam he keeps under the front seat so it sort of evens out maybe. Once they got to asking questions they might want to know if any of that Schedule

20 stainless pipe that was short on the last inventory and that Mr. Hansen wouldn't stop bitching about was maybe under a tarp back of somebody's garage and I don't have a garage.

I was fired and all that shit, who's surprised? But I came back a couple weeks later to eat lunch with the guys 'cause I thought Wally might help me find another job for keeping my mouth shut and all, but I saw that wasn't never going to happen. Before we even got to the break room, I was standing next to him at the urinal, and he nodded up at the ceiling with his chin and said, It must suck to be the asshole who has to sit all day and watch us pee.

I said, Wha'?

And he said, Since you left they been watching us all the time. Wired the whole damn place, putting in cameras. Didn't make no secret of it.

But they can't do it in here, can they?

Not *legally*.

So for help I went to Brenda, the blonde girl I was chasing then and not getting much of nowhere—hair so white it looked fake because it was fake, but hell she was trying. She helped me get on doing night cleanup at Hendry's IGA and that wasn't so bad because it's small and the butchers do all their own cleanup. That's the worst stuff mostly, 'cept for the toilets, and ain't but two of those and they aren't for customers, so you know who's using them and they know you know, and I don't mind calling them out about piss on the floor if I have to. So I ate pretty good for a couple of months going toward spring—mostly just sliced bread and lunch meat, nothing too big—when I started seeing this little brunette. Bit of a mistake that one, freckly girl, single again at forty and ready for it though she moaned a lot about when was I going to sleep over at her house like I was all excited about walking out of her bedroom in the morning and grinning an I-been-boning-your-mom grin at a seventeen-year-old boy forty pounds bigger than me and lettering in football and felonious assault. Brenda didn't get me fired about the brunette, but she did put the night manager on alert so I had to start buying my own food, which was like taking a pay cut.

But here's the whole point I've been getting to, which was that I brought Brenda, once we got back together for a while, to Fourth of July at my rich cousin Robert's place out in the country because it was his turn and he owns his house. Been Bobby till he got to high school, then he was Bob. But go to law school and make a fortune putting criminals back on the street and you become Robert and don't have to listen when somebody calls you Bobby even though he drug you out of your granddaddy's oak tree when your ladder fell over and you'd been up there crying for three hours like a baby. Even fetched down his damn windup plastic airplane for his little crybaby ass.

They set us at a porch table with the children and Stevey, and his wife whose name I never can remember, something like Will Fred. That's not it exactly, but it's what I call her. She answers to it. And just as soon as I took a big bite of rich-cousin hamburger and started chewing, Stevey says in that slow retarded way of his, I wan you stop tell people I retarded.

I never told no one you a retard, Stevey, I said, and Brenda looked at me funny, which reminded me I had told her and done a little imitation too, which she didn't like but her brothers laughed at it pretty good.

Let's be clear here. Stevey *is* a retard. He worked in the sheltered workshop for a year—it's where he met his wife—before they got him that job at Circle K he's had for like ten years. Daddy always said Stevey had a certificate from the state proving he was a retard but I've never seen it. It's not exactly something you bring out when rich cousin Robert is showing everybody *Winesburg Argus* clippings about every base hit his boy made or the ribbons his girls won in horse jumping.

Mr. Smuh, Smuh, Smuh—Mr. Smitherman at work tole me you tole ev'body at your work I wah retard.

Then Mr. Smuh's a liar.

He said I han't drop pah, pah, pallet TVs.

The retard wife and the kids at the table started giggling till I stood up, and just as I was trying to decide if I should hit him or kick the table over, Robert put his hand on my shoulder and said, Why don't you do what Steve asks and not talk about him. That'd be like a kindness to everyone, don't you think? Let's go see if there's another one of those—whatcha got there, Molsons? So I picked up the rest of my burger and followed him to get a beer I didn't have much taste for anymore because he was right that you shouldn't torment the less fortunate. I did motion Brenda in front of me, gentleman like, before I turned back and kinda swept my eyes over Stevey and Will Fred and them kids too so they'd know Uncle Ray hadn't forgot nothing. Over by the beer tub, I could tell Robert wanted to say something more, so I just took a couple of Molsons in each hand and led Brenda straight to the truck. Told Brenda she should take a couple too but she said, No, I don't think so.

Ken of Ottumwa

Every fall, I visit all the schools in Winesburg to make the pictures.
I make the class pictures. I make the individual pictures of each
individual student. I make the pictures of the teachers. And even
the staff (the janitors, the lunch ladies, the secretaries, the crossing guards, the school nurses), I make their pictures too. I take my
camera to the Emile Durkheim High School (the public school),
St. Edward the Confessor Roman Catholic School, Martin Lu-
ther Lutheran School. Every year, I make all the pictures in all
these schools. I make the pictures for the Richard Corey technical
school and the Edward Everett Hale, and the Sullivans junior high
schools. And I make pictures for the elementary schools (Lincoln,
Garfield, McKinley, and Kennedy). Every fall, I make a lot of pictures. And each sitting gets four takes (at least). Everyone gets four
tries to make the picture I make come out right.

My wife, Clare, works with me in all the schools on the day
we make the pictures. She brings with her the big tackle box of
makeup, the jars of hair gel and cans of hair spray, the bobby pins
and barrettes, and plenty of mirrors. We don't tell the subjects but
the mirrors are trick ones, just a little bit, to flatter their faces, make
them thinner, smoother, younger, older. My wife hands out the
free hard-rubber pocket combs imprinted with "Ken of Ottumwa

Studio" on one side of the handle and "Ace" on the other. She watches the students in the hallway outside the door to the backstage of the cafetorium where I have set up my temporary studio. All of the children combing and combing their hair, licking their fingers to smooth down cowlick after cowlick. I can hear my wife calm them down. You are lovely, she says. You have a beautiful smile. She says, this is your best side. I believe that school photograph day creates more anxiety than any test. It is, after all, a measure of who they have become, all the making up of the lives they are making up captured here at this moment. I hear her coax and cajole as I set up the scoop lights and strobes, charge the batteries, adjust the backdrop (it is silver white for all the school pictures though back at the studio I have a variety of backgrounds—the Grand Canyon, the heavy red velvet drapery, the bookshelf filled with books, the end zone of the old RCA Dome), organize the rolls of film (I still use film) with the charts filled with the names of the students waiting outside. Heaven forbid that Ken of Ottumwa would mix up the photographs, caption one picture with the wrong name. No, the kids as they arrange their hair, as they button and unbutton their blouses and shirts, as they remove their glasses, as they smile hard at each other examining each other's teeth—they carry with them a slip of paper with their name and address and a serial number for me to match with the four frames (at least!) that will be allotted to them. The money is in the packages I sell to them—all the different combinations of 8×10s, 5×7s, 3½×5s, the wallet sizes, the size for grandparents who will frame the portraits, the postage stamp size for trading with friends. None of the packages make any sense. Everyone always ends up with too many of at least one kind. They get proofs. The four (at least) poses where they try, try, try, try to picture the you that is you (my motto). There is always one half-lidded take or one with the eyes closed altogether, one all apout when she wanted to smile, one all teeth when he wanted to be tight-lipped. Don't get me started on cheese, on the banter I must recite day in and day out, the counting up to the moment I trip the shutter, the stutter as the lights flashing hit the subject. How I must prop him up again as he blinks uncontrollably. How I nicker at her as her irises gyrate and jump. The confusions of my lefts and your rights, the jumbling of movable body parts (the eyes looking up, the chin down, the head turned, the shoulder pulled back). And the smile, smile, smile, smile. The look here, look here, look here, look here. My wife Clare also helps the seniors with the break front formal gowns, the fake strand of pearls, the tuxedo bib, and clip-on bow. The costumes are soaked through by the end of that day's shooting, and we spray it down with the same stuff they use for shoes at the bowling alley. Recently, the anxiety in line has gotten even more compounded and confused as most of the students (even the kindergarteners) carry surreptitious cell phones bundled with their own digital cameras. They are not supposed to have them in school but in the hallway milling, waiting, nervous, bored, their teachers distracted by their own vanities, they turn on their phones, flipping them up like old-fashioned compact mirrors accompanied by little songs that twinkle like old music boxes. They make each other's pictures. They make pictures of each other. They make pictures of each other making pictures. They make pictures of each other making pictures of each other. And then (I know it) they begin sending the pictures they have made to each other. I can hear the phones ringing, singing, buzzing, clicking as they receive the pictures. I can feel them, the pictures, being sent in the air around me like the floating after-images of all the real pictures I make of the same children on the spinning piano stool in front of the silver-white background strobing on the excited filmy film of my retina. Back in the darkroom I drift around in the dark feeling my way around, around the vats of chemicals, the boxes of paper. I crack open the yellow canisters of spent film like eggs. I spool up rolls and rolls and rolls and rolls of film, bathing them like bars of soap in soapy water. The filmstrips spiral and drip-dry in viney jungle clumps around the room. I spend days enlarging the negatives onto the undeveloped swatches of blank paper. My wife Clare helps me here in the dark in the flashing light of the enlarger enlarging, in the diffuse candling safety light. I make pictures the old way with the sweet-smelling chemicals and the balsamic fixing baths, the big stop clocks ticking always ticking, the squeegee squeegeeing. Clare, my wife, and I do some dodging and burning, some over- and underexposing. We crop. We pull focus. I watch her making the pictures, all the techniques of retouching, smoothing the surface of a forehead, plucking an eyebrow, smoothing a cheek, pearling a tooth. She drips a dollop of white paint in an eye recreating the flash of my lights when the picture was made. All of this to give depth to the flat flat flat flatness of the pictures. Shadows and perspective, chiaroscuro with the airbrush's air compressor hissing hissing. We score with the wax pencil. We measure the grainy graininess of the flesh, our eyes pressed into the loops. What will they become? These thems? What will we make of them? What will they make of themselves? I know one day (if we stay in the business) I will need to switch over to the digital pixels, the alternating codes, the electronic genetics, the ones and zeros. But, for now, we watch together (under the safety light) the incubation, the development, the emergence, the revelation of each face, face, face, face, before our eyes, beginning with their eyes opening, opening in the depthless depths of those white white fields.

Miss Gladys

Mornings, this autumn, I see the girls skipping past on their way to school, and my heart lifts at the sound of their bright voices. I live at the end of Locust Street in a one-story frame house with a porch that wraps around the side. If visitors know me, they knock on the side door when they come, aware that I spend most of my time in the dining room where I have my television set and the oak drop-leaf table I inherited from my mother, and the rocking chair, reupholstered now, that belonged to my father. I sit at the table working a crossword. The television is on for the noise, usually some sort of news show on CNN because I like to keep up to date. I may be on the far side of eighty, but I'm not dead yet. The world can still amaze me.

This morning, I hear a voice outside my window—a light, thin voice singing that old kids' song, "Itsy Bitsy Spider." I glance up from my puzzle, and I see the girl, no more than nine or ten, coming up the steps toward my front door. It's one of those cloudless September days when the air is so clear, the slightest sound carries. Crows caw from the oak trees where the leaves are just now tinged with red. A car door slams somewhere up the street. The last bell rings at Garfield Elementary, where once upon a time I taught, and I hear it plain as day.

"You're late for school," I say to the girl when I open the front door.

"I'm on my way," she says, not flustered a bit, and for a moment I remember the girl I was, head in the stars, chin leading forward, ready to make my life.

"You want to buy this?" She holds on her palm a figurine made from spun glass, a pale blue hummingbird, wings open, its beak probing a petunia bloom. The beak is short and too flat. The bird's eyes are too far apart, and, well, truth be told, the whole thing is a mess. The head is too big, the body too arched in an attempt to make it seem that the bird is hovering over the petunia. The bird actually seems to be smiling, and I can't decide whether it looks more like a dolphin or a maybe a cross between a dolphin and a platypus. "My daddy made it," the girl says.

"Does your daddy need glasses?" I can't help myself. It's said before I can stop it. "You ought to get to school."

The girl tips back her head a tad, squints at me, then says in a very measured voice, "You ought not to be such a mean old bitch."

Maybe I fall in love with her a little, as much charmed as I am shocked by how she comes back at me like that. What can I do but buy the figurine—five dollars, she wants for it.

"What are you going to do with that money?" I ask her.

She folds the bill and sticks it into her jacket pocket. It's a thin denim jacket, short in the waist, and faded from too many washings. Frayed threads, nearly white, unravel from the collar and the cuffs. She stuffs her fists into her pockets and shrugs her shoulders—such a slight, delicate girl with a long neck and fine blonde hair, blue veins showing through the white skin of her eyelids.

"Guess I'll know that when I've got enough," she says.

She smells like old cooking oil and black bananas and wet dirt. I can't place her from any of the houses nearby; could be she lives in one of the trailers the next street over. A smudge of something dark shadows the left corner of her mouth. When she catches me looking at that stain with a disapproving frown, she tucks her head down and rubs her jaw across her shoulder.

"How will you know when you have enough?"

She shrugs again. "Just will. You want me to come back tomorrow?" She smiles at me so sweetly. "I'll bring you another pretty."

"And want another five dollars, I suppose?"

She doesn't flinch. "Pretty is as pretty costs."

"You think five dollars makes that hummingbird look any less like a platypus?"

I don't let her know that she's shaken me. My breath is catching in my throat. I feel like my legs might give way. I've only heard someone change up that old saw about pretty is as pretty does one other time in my life, but now this girl has said it—pretty is as pretty *costs*—and just like that I'm back over sixty years ago in the cafe by the Winesburg train station—the White Spot—and I've just ordered a piece of coconut cream pie.

It was August, the dog days, and I was having lunch before going back to my summer job at the Rexall drugstore. I worked the cash register and stocked shelves when business was slow. Sometimes I delivered medicines to customers who were housebound, folks as old as I am now. The pharmacist, Mr. Lister, called me his girl. "I'll send my girl right over with your heart pills," he'd tell someone on the phone. "What's that? Oh, yes, she's a good girl. Very dependable. She'll be there in a jiff."

That day at the White Spot, I was bored, and only a week away from the end of that summer job. I was eager to be back at Oakland City College, where I was studying to be an elementary school teacher. All summer, as customers had come and gone, I'd felt

Winesburg close around me. My job gave me too much intimacy with people and their infirmities and habits. I knew who suffered from gout, lumbago, insomnia, heart palpitations, dyspepsia, toenail fungus, athlete's foot, ringworm, vertigo. I knew the women who colored their hair, the teenagers who smoked Chesterfields and Pall Malls, the men who wore trusses and sometimes took penicillin for matters better left undisclosed. I knew all this, and it was too much to know. It left me longing for someone who could be a mystery to me, someone I could know a little bit at a time and never feel like I knew everything.

Then I ordered that piece of coconut cream pie, and the waitress, Meryl Lane, who came into the Rexall each month to buy the new *True Confessions* magazine—she'd been reading the August issue when I'd sat down at the lunch counter; I'd seen it open to an article entitled, "I Couldn't Forgive My Brother-in-Law"—told me that the man at the other end of the lunch counter had just ordered the last piece of pie. A man in a light blue seersucker suit and a red and navy bowtie. A stranger with a yellow-cream leather suitcase on the floor by his stool. A pretty man with black hair, oiled and combed. He looked at me and smiled, and I felt my heart go.

"Why don't we split it?" he said. "Go halvsies. You game?"

I was indeed. I picked up my hatbox pocketbook, let it swing in my hand by its Lucite handle, and strolled down the line of counter stools. My dress was new, a lavender summer dress with white polka dots, and a circle skirt with a ruffled hem. I liked the way the ruched bust flattered me, and I hoped this man would like it, too. I took my time as if I knew exactly where I was going and didn't need to hurry.

Turned out, I didn't know a thing.

A piece of coconut cream pie. A man with time to kill while he waited on his train, a girl with her head in the clouds and eager for her real life to begin.

I stand here now toward the end of that life, and I can remember the way the air felt when the man and I stepped outside the White Spot—heavy with humidity, the sky overcast, and everything so still the way it is when a storm is coming. Locusts chirred. The couplings of boxcars clanked together in the rail yards behind the station. A smell of old flowers and dried cornstalks and river water told me autumn was coming soon.

What did we do? That man and I? I took his hand. I led him down the alley and up the stairs to the room above the Rexall that Mr. Lister used for storage. I shut the door behind us, and I didn't turn on the light.

The man set down his yellow-cream suitcase.

"Do you like my dress?" I said. "Do you think it's pretty?"

He moved in close to me. He put his hands on my waist. "Pretty is as pretty costs," he said.

He moved his hand up under my skirt, and I let him. I didn't know everything that would follow. I didn't know that my life had already started to change. I didn't know that come spring, I'd be at the Nebraska Children's Home in Omaha, saying goodbye to my newborn daughter. I didn't know I'd never marry, didn't know I'd spend my life taking care of other women's children. To me, it was just a late-summer afternoon in Winesburg. I was just an antsy girl, too daring for her own good, too brazen. I had my whole life ahead of me.

Now, the girl at my house looks up at me, her chin quivering and turning to gooseflesh. "It's a hummingbird," she says. "A goddamn hummingbird. Are you blind? Anyone can see that."

I tell her to come back tomorrow, and to bring me another pretty. "I'll pay." She turns and runs down my steps, up the sidewalk to school. All I can do is step out onto my porch and call after her. "You just tell me how much." I watch until I can't see her anymore. "I'll pay whatever it costs."

But she's gone, so I go back into my dining room, where I set the hummingbird figurine on top of my television.

CNN tells me that the United Nations will try to resolve the Syrian government's bloody offensive against its citizens; unease continues in Egypt; the rapper 50 Cent is visiting impoverished sites in Kenya and Somalia; Human Rights Watch calls for Iraqi officials to stop executing prisoners; the Mexican army has seized more than fifteen tons of methamphetamine from a clandestine laboratory in a remote area of the state of Jalisco.

Meanwhile, I'm living through another day in Winesburg, already thinking about bedtime when I'll lie down to sleep. I like to let the world get by on its own for a few hours, but sometimes I think about the man with the yellow-cream suitcase and the daughter he never knew existed. I hope she has a happy life. I hope the thought of me doesn't bear upon her. I say a little prayer for her, and one for the girl with the hummingbird figurine. Then I let it all go—the things I can't change—and all morning I watch the way the sunlight splinters through the spun glass of that figurine, sending spots of color wheeling across my floor, my wall. I almost believe I can reach out and hold them in my hand.

The Processed
Cheese Product Man

Sunday is clear and the night comes on warm and pleasant. Monday a yellow chariot clatters into town. It is a double-wide.

❋   ❋   ❋

An awkward introduction. (It will be a story worth telling someday.) As a newcomer, Amos is jumpy about his jumpy laugh. Does it frighten others? Are the locals going to say it's a cackle? The term *cackle* holds character implications. Amos considers: Do I carry a strange and sour odor on my clothing, hands, on my hair?

A tall man with a small tomato balanced atop his derby hat arrives at the chariot. He removes the derby, bows, hands the tomato to Amos, and says, "A man of conceptuals like you needs to see the Mayor."

On the way to the Mayor, the tall man chatters along like a squirrel: "Processed Cheese Product now. A lot might be done with Processed Cheese Product, eh? It's almost inconceivable. I mean to think about it. The conceptuals of you and the Mayor thinking about it. There would be a new classification, you see. It's interesting, eh? It's conceptuals, like I said. Wait till you see the Mayor, he'll get the conceptuals. He'll be interested. The Mayor is always interested in the conceptuals. You can't be too smart for the Mayor, now can you? Of course you can't. You know that."

They stand together on the front porch of the dry goods store, the Mayor and Amos. Where did the tall man go? I'll tell you: He folded himself down onto the ground, lengthwise, then shuffled his lanky body beneath the planking of the store. Apparently, he prefers to live his life low.

"Well I guess that there chariot is just farting out jobs," the Mayor says. A woman in a red bikini rides a bicycle past. She waves at the men. Three scrawny cows walk by, slowly. They appear to be drugged. The sun is low and wide and all flattened out in the upkicked dust. Brown.

Inside the store we find cacophony: a spreading and processing and distilling and tasting. A smelting and a hardening and an expo. A strange aroma mingles with the room's other smells: a bit musty, somewhat like burning leaves, copper-tinged. Painted tin harmonicas stuffed with Processed Cheese Product are handed out as keepsakes. Word spreads. Children pushing lumps of Processed Cheese Product across the floor. Men tucking three, four harmonicas down their sleeves. Several Dry Plate Glass Negatives. The Mayor's cheeks are swollen with Processed Cheese Product, red, glistening, sweaty hamster. Men roll it into cigars. Children form it into ineffective slingshots. Someone bounces a ball. Even Mrs. Dorothy Philomena Chandler takes a bite, well, a nibble. "That tastes like witchcraft," she says.

In the center of this rattle and thump, something is drifting inside Amos. His thoughts as orange asterisks on the wind. On the window glass, the tin roof, stuck there, smeared. On the dusty floor. Okay, I'll say it—Amos is a bit of a depressive. He imagines he feels himself aging. As Amos holds high an artist's rendition of a Reincorporator "facilitating the curd," his fingers become less sensitive to touch. He drops a full tin can of V-Cola onto the town's only Player Banjo. Amos senses that his actual skin cells are gradually losing their elasticity. It's not so funny.

※ ※ ※

"*I* want to *sit* in the *front* of the *fucking* Reincorporator," says Sara on Tuesday. Her bike leans against a claw-foot bathtub. (The bathtub tucked inside a clever carpentry appendage of the chariot.)

※ ※ ※

On Wednesday the Flattner/Loader Amos erected down by the creek screeches like a zoo animal and tumbles over. Someone—or something—has removed the leg bolts. The wind is up now, dust spinning, and the birds are spiraling in the drafts. Birds Amos generally admires, though he does dislike the raven because of its intellect. The pure dazzle of its impertinent mind. Sometimes Amos feels that ravens watch his every move, and he is pleased to see them sketch away into the sky. "Did you even know young ravens form gangs?" Amos lectures the Sticker-Slappers, slow, young farmhands all. "They actually recruit one another. Then they go around stealing everyone's cheese."

Amos tells himself he enjoys lecturing the youth. He climbs a pile of railroad ties and shouts most any variety of advice—birds, molasses recipes, wooden silverware, the proper method for constructing a rectangle, etc.—until his voice cracks and everyone drifts away. Then Amos sits on the railroad ties, his legs warm against the pitch. He thinks, Where does the wind go, where has it been? A bit whimsical on the afterwash of Public Speech and the odor of WD-40, he is reminded of voices from his childhood, or of Velveeta ("Only the few know the sweetness of the twisted cheese," Amos is prone to say), his favorite Processed Cheese Product. Those that change, but do not.

✳   ✳   ✳

On Thursday Sara just walks through the kitchen of the yellow chariot, naked. It makes Amos's thoughts collapse, then helix into staircases of orange foam. To wit: Finding God in a woman. Fortunately or unfortunately. Sara is much like the underdog letters of the alphabet. That cunning and exponential. That powerful, really.

Amos's favorite bird is the mockingbird.

✳   ✳   ✳

The packaging of Velveeta has changed over the years, but so has Amos. Look at the Dry Plate Glass Negatives. (Everyone, as you know, smiles in the Dry Plate Glass Negatives, a profound thought on my part, a thought that could spawn pages and pages, arguments and essays and fictional representations . . . Or really just a trivial observation, this Dry Plate Glass Negatives/smile thing, so ordinary as to even bore a butterfly.) Listen: Like everyone, Amos once wanted to be a sculptor, then time passed and all his limbs shortened and his hair fell to the floor, while deposits of fat filled in the center of his torso (also his skin deteriorated, as I have mentioned). Like everyone, Amos wakes in the middle of the night and takes long showers in his chariot's Shower Chamber and grabs the neck of the showerhead and cries directly into the face of the dark spray. Amos? He appreciates etherized June bugs, pound cake, bright, primary colors, WD-40, science fairs (the roar and rattle of industry), the pleasurable annoyance of an afternoon repairing a wobbly Flattner.

Shall we return to the railroad ties?

"What town am I in? Muncie or Memphis? I don't remember and anyway it makes no difference. Oh one day all of you will appreciate the ways and words of Velveeta, its voice, its vision, the actual phrasings, the colloquialisms, the intuitive art of storytelling—you just don't hear those types of sounds anymore. Is anyone listening? Is anyone alive in this town? Velveeta has no known expiration date!"

And the workers drift away . . .

✳   ✳   ✳

Friday. Fourteen flaming jars of mayonnaise shatter the windows of the temporary Whey Station. Inside the jars are notes written on husks of corn. Amos squints at the letterings:

1. LET HER BE OR I WILL HOLD A FAT FACE TIGHTLY AGAINST YOUR PILLOW. I AM NOT A COWARD.

2. GOD VOMITED THE DAYS YOU WERE BERN

3. SHINY AND YELLOW FELLOW

4. MOST OF US NEED BRITCHES AND YOU HAVE LOTS OF BRITCHES IT SEEMS LIKELY

5. LOVE IS SPECTRE FOLKS BABBLE ABOUT NOT EVEN ONCE SEEN!

6. I WILL HURL YOU LIKE THE WIND INTO THE BERRY BUSHES

7. WHAT CHARIOT?

8. I FED THE FERRETS EVERY DAY THE VEVELVETVA AS YOU INSTRUCTED AND NOW IT HAS DIED!

9. MAN OF AFFAIRS! BIGGITY MAN OF AFFAIRS!

10. ON THE BEST DAYS MY HEART THE SIZE OF A GRAPE. NOW THAT YOU IS NEAR MY HEART THE SIZE OF A RAISIN

11. I AM NEVER MAKING OUT WHAT YOU ARE SAYING WHEN YOU SPEAK TO ME SO PLEASE LEAVE THIS TOWN OR TALK LIKE GOD MEANT US TO TALK YOU SAM WITCH

12. UNHAND HER!

13. I AM WONDERING MR. AMOS IF YOU COULD CREATE A MAN OUT OF YOUR CHEESE? MEET ME BY THE COWS BY THE CORN BY THE FERRIS WHEEL ON THOSE FLAT BOARDS

14. THINGS ARE TRENDING TO SMASH

❋ ❋ ❋

Amos just keeps staring at Sara. Staring and staring. Amos is trying to capture her, to fix her in place. Minutes pass. Amos is most likely creeping her out. Finally, she puts down her Velveeta (she was billowing it—a recent hobby). She says, "What?" Amos says, "Nothing." She goes back to billowing her Velveeta, and Amos just keeps on staring.

✳ ✳ ✳

The sky that fateful evening? Well, as you know, my friends, there was a disturbance. It banged and clanged, remember? A tempest of some kind, certainly. Footsteps or thunder? Pitchforks or lightning? Voices or . . . the wind howling and the rain sweeping across the roof and the air full of electricity and then everything falling away. Some form of large, round sign was lifted from the tin roof of the dry goods store, and, you know, dropped onto Amos's chariot. Big-ass orange sign. Strange: Amos arrives from the East; a fierce storm arrives from the West. They join in Winesburg. But I digress . . . the sky . . . the actual sky: horizontal stripes, jagged clouds. Tinted dark blue shot with yellow silver. Not so unlike the spinning blades of a Reincorporator.

✳ ✳ ✳

Saturday, in the quiet after, the ravens return and remove every clothespin from the laundry line running between the chariot's flagpole and the apex of the Curd Silo. (Ravens are incredibly nimble, especially with their talons and beaks, and can easily bend Time/construct mosaics/brew coffee/open doors/laugh/grimace/howl/presurmise/seep or pang or suck or fuck or plop/write lives/rearrange lives/erase lives/fictionalize with a vengeance/etch with steam/fit pearls into sockets/fetch weapons or late trains/plant, grow, pluck varieties of berries/play cards or phonograph or Reincorporate without violent retch/repair clocks and/or leaden windows/fall into buckets of corn/shave or pop or lop corn for winter drinks [liquor]/grind corn/melt corn/leap into barricades/bloom like unhinged syllables into the air/love/un-love/cry/sing.)

Now Amos's clothing lies there, empty and rumpled on the ground, like a group of fallen dead, the bodies raptured away.

❋ ❋ ❋

On Sunday we arrive at the end of Amos's story. A fat woman disembarks from a train. She waddles right up to the Mayor and says, "Where's Amos Jefferson Pyle? I am his wife."

Sara looks at the Mayor. (Oddly, Sara is sitting on the Mayor's lap. Her rippling orange dress covers both their legs.) The Mayor removes a bright pink harmonica from his breast pocket, attempts a little, lilting ditty, but the notes fall away. Returning the harmonica to his breast pocket, he sighs. Then says, "Who?"

Burt Coble, Catman

Yeah, I seen your little town at night. It's usually me and the moon coming up through there about three, four in the morning, boat on the squeaking trailer behind me, still dripping green river water from its bunks, and I notice your Dollar General lit up for safety, pole lights shining down on the empty yellow lines, feral cats slinking around the Dairymart, and one or two cars of high schoolers still hustling split-tail in the parking lot of the school. Used to be every buck wanted his Cutlass jacked up on air shocks. That or a lifted four-by-four. Now about every kid I see gots a foreign job, all lowered so the bumpers scrape pulling into the post office. 'Course, what's kids today got to mail anyway? But one more thing on them feral cats: more than once, I seen two or three tomcats circling an old mama cat in heat. They say a cat screams like it does when it's getting mated because a tomcat has a barbed penis. They also tell you a possum has a forked penis, but I don't even know how something like that would work. But yeah, I seen your houses all dark, everybody inside sleeping away, drooling on pillows. I know which places got them little baby blues, cause I see the light on low in some corner, mama rocking her baby don't want to sleep. I seen all that and more.

Once I slowed down to watch two farm boys whaling on each other outside the White Spot. Some young thing in a skirt watching them, bouncing on her feet, hands up by her throat. Another time I seen a woman stumbling right down the middle of the street, drunk enough to grease-bump with an old boy like me, even after I been fishing all night, but I wasn't much in the mood for it. I just slowed down and drove 'round her. I done got enough for someone old enough to remember this town before Dairy Queen, if you get me. Lots of times I pass a woman driving home all alone after giving her man some mud for his turtle. Sometimes it's the man's head silhouetted in a cab, especially if his new lady got a man or if he got another woman back at his place. I know a little something about how that works. It calls for a schedule and it pays to know when folks get off work.

What this town does when the decent folks go to sleep after switching off the news would tighten the guide-wires of some Winesburgers and tighten the pants of some others. I seen what this town does to itself in the blue-black night. Them new mamas could see it, too, but they don't focus on nothing but their crying babies. For that I don't blame them. I had three kids and I never was the one getting up with them but I know for a fact it takes a toll on a person. And most everybody else who could see these happenings is either doing it or is too drunk or both. The cop? You know you're pissing on my back and calling it rain with that one. I know where he parks after midnight, out behind the propane tanks at 101 and Main, and I don't know why they ever give them boys computers, 'cause when I go by there, trailer rattle-ta-tattle banging and squeaking, he don't even look up, his face lit with the glow from his computer. I don't doubt but that he plays games on it or looks at pictures of naked women.

Speaking of naked women, back before my hair was gray I knew a woman married to a guy used to work graveyard up there at Allison Transmission. He'd head to the line about midnight and I'd jump in the truck and slide over there to visit his lady, a woman named Lila with hair black as a crow's back. Back then no one had cell phones and no one checked in with no one at any time, didn't seem like. Lila's man'd drive off and never wonder but that his old lady was home sawing logs in that big log house by herself. Not true.

During that same period of my life there was a woman I called Squeaky married to a man got real sick with cancer and was laid up in the big hospital up there in Danville. From what I was told, one leg damn near rotted off his trunk. I know what you're thinking: it's a terrible sinful man who'd pay nighttime visits to a woman with a husband getting ate up from the cancer. In my defense let me say this: I never once called her. Night after night, it was her calling me. In fairness to her reputation after about one week of us carrying on, didn't neither one of us need to call. I'd just show up with a case of beer and a pigsticker I had just rinsed off with rubbing alcohol for safety. Talk about cold.

If you see me out in the broad sunlight, you ought to take a picture, because I ain't never been one for high noon. They say if you see a raccoon out in the daylight, you better shoot it, because it's sick in the head. Same goes for me, bar the shooting part. Been lots of nights I half-expected to get shot coming out of someone's house but I guess I was borned lucky.

Now days I don't hardly carry on with no women. I know I never got less ornery, I know that. Anymore I just fish the White River down by Centerton Road and I get my bluegills as the sun sets and fish the big flatties till they stop biting for sure at two or three. That's another one of them different world things, you could say, 'cause it's just me out there on the water, sitting still in my old green flatbottom, the moon rising up over the trees and hitting the water like sparks from a welder, but softer, like they falling through rain, even when it's not, the water all around you moving slow and stinking like a dinosaur swamp. I hook them bluegills through the back behind the spiny fin and when I cast them out they tremble and fight against the line till a big cat swoops in and eats 'em. Very little sound at all except for the night birds and then the boomslap when a beaver sees my boat and smacks his tail down on the water.

Some nights I sit out there till the sun comes up and I can see the world around me again. Other nights I knock off in the blue hours and trailer the boat, then drive slowly through the pot-chucked streets of this little town. I drive real slow and look in them houses and watch for windows showing some sign of life. Just to feel the old urge. Maybe a light, maybe a shadow of some-one moving behind a thin curtain of gauze. I know some of them windows. Some of them I looked out of a time or two. I know for a straight cold fact there's some lonely women in this town.

Tara Jenkins

I knew I loved Melissa in the second grade because she was always so serious, her gray eyes locked on whatever she was looking at like it was the only thing in the world. One day, her eyes locked on me, and I knew she wasn't ever going to let me go. I didn't want her to. Me and Melissa, we were always going to be something.

I knew I loved Melissa in the eighth grade when we were in her room, the door sealed shut from her mom and dad and my mom and dad and all our brothers and their mess. After school, we lay on her bed on our stomachs, everything about us flat. The music was loud; her mother yelled at us through the door but her mother never came in so we never turned it down. We talked under the music and let our shoulders touch, creating this perfect place where our bodies met. The quieter we got and the more we cut ourselves open for each other, baring our secret selves, the warmer that place between us grew until it made our skin soft and eventually that place burned. It was nothing but it was everything. We'd pull away and face each other and our lips would quiver but we were too scared to do anything and finally, when it was too much to see each other so plainly she would say, real quiet like, "You better go," and just when I got up to leave she'd grab my hand and say, "You better stay."

Everyone in Winesburg always said I was the pretty one, the girl who could go to some impossible place like New York City and make something of her smile. Melissa was as pretty as me but no one could see it because they didn't want to really look at her. She wore her hair on the top of her head most of the time, and would probably get buried in a pair of jeans if she had her way. She didn't feel the need to show off for anyone. I'm the only person who has ever seen the best parts of her, like she was saving those best parts for me.

I knew I loved Melissa in the ninth grade when I dated Tom Pederson. He chewed tobacco, chewed so much his jaw always hurt. He liked it when I let him put his head in my lap and I would rub my fingers over his jawbone in slow, steady circles while he sighed. When he kissed me, he tasted like mint and grit. After our dates, I'd go to Melissa's. She'd be real cold to me for the first while, snapping, being mean. She'd sit on the edge of her bed, every part of her stiff, one angry line of body and bone. I'd sit next to her and wait her anger out. Eventually, she'd say, "You stink like him." I needed to tell her, "I want to stink like you," but we didn't have the right words, not for her to explain why she was mad, or for me to explain why I liked that she was mad.

Melissa wasn't like me. She was never going to let some dirty Winesburg boy touch her or walk her to class or take her to the drive-in or any of that. All she ever wanted was me and for us to be our own family. She didn't think it was possible, not for us, not in our town. Sometimes, when we lay in her bed, she'd pull my hand onto her stomach and she'd sigh and talk about babies and she'd sound so lonesome. I'd wish I could fill her empty places.

She didn't understand we were exactly the same. When I went out with a boy, it didn't mean anything. I don't even know why I did it.

Actually, I do know why I did it. I was seventeen when a boy named Klaus knocked me up. He was a farmer like his daddy, two years older than me. The first time I met him, we were outside the hardware store and he was throwing some big ole bags of something into the back of his beat-up Chevy. I looked at him and said, "Your neck is actually red." He stopped what he was doing, letting the bag of something in his hands hang, the burlap stretching from the weight of gravity until finally he let it fall to the ground. He leaned against the truck, stretching one leg toward me. He said, "You sure don't have any manners, do you?" I shrugged and leaned against his truck, too. I said, "That depends on what you call manners." He took me to dinner in Terre Haute and acted like this was the nicest thing he was ever going to do in his whole life. I don't even remember what we talked about. I thought of Melissa and how when we were alone, she took her hair down, and I was the only one who ever got to see all of her, open and loose. I thought of Melissa when Klaus kissed me in the parking lot of the restaurant that night and when he fumbled, trying to push my skirt up around my hips when we lay in the back of his pickup and when I wrapped my arms around him while I stared up at the sky wishing it wasn't cloudy.

Melissa knew I was pregnant before I did. I was feeling terrible for weeks, every part of me swollen with water and tender to the touch. I couldn't keep anything down and after school I'd fall asleep on her bed while she did homework, tap tap tapping away at the keyboard, humming some song. She loves to hum, no matter what she's doing, there's some kind of song on her breath. One day, I woke up nauseous, my stomach rolling and rolling. She turned to look at me and she said, "You're pregnant," and I said, "I am?" She shook her head. "I can't believe you fucked him." I went to her, fell to my knees and lay my head in her lap, the way Tom Pederson used to do to me. "I let him fuck me," I said. "There's a difference." But Melissa didn't reach for me, wouldn't touch me, and then I reached for her trash can and threw up.

I told Melissa I was having the baby for her because I knew she wasn't going to let some boy fuck her. She didn't believe me. She said mean things she shouldn't have said. Then she stopped talking to me entirely. I'd knock on her door but she wouldn't answer. Her mother said, "Melissa doesn't want to see you," and sent me on my way. At school, Melissa ignored me, but I'd feel her watching me walk to class and walk to class and walk to class, my belly growing bigger and bigger. At home, I'd sit in my room waiting for her to pick up the phone, my parents pretending I was a different kind of girl who didn't bring them another baby to raise. Klaus called sometimes, but I ignored him. He would have loved me if I let him but I didn't.

I told Klaus me and the baby were going to be fine. I told him he could be a daddy if he wanted but we weren't going to be like our parents, living like ghosts, doing what other folks thought was right. I told him my heart was already tied up in someone else, always had been, always would be, and that I wasn't going to un-tangle those bloody knots. He stared at me while I talked, his big hands held open like he was trying to catch something he couldn't quite hold on to. Finally he shook his head, said, "This doesn't feel right," and I put my hand on his shoulder. I said, "We'll figure out a way to make this right for us."

It took longer than I thought for Melissa to come around, so long I started to think I had finally pushed her too far. The way she stared through me, like I wasn't even there—it made it hard for me to breathe, made my chest tighten in the worst way. When I was eight months gone, my ankles started swelling and I had to wear my Converse every day. I'd trudge through school, hot and fat and sweaty, feeling like I had no one in the world but a baby that no one but me wanted.

I knew I loved Melissa on an afternoon in April when it was crazy hot like summer. I was walking across the front lawn after Calculus trying to make sense of polynomials and how they approximate other functions or whatever it was Mr. Frankel said in class. The baby was kicking at me. It didn't hurt but it didn't feel good either. Everyone around me was being normal and young and enjoying the warm weather and there was a baseball game that night so people were excited because Winesburg doesn't have much but we do have a good baseball team.

Melissa passed by. She looked right through me the way she had for months. She looked at me like there was nothing between us; she stole the rest of my fire.

I fell to the ground right there. I didn't care. It was cooler on the ground, but not much. Sweat pooled between my breasts and in the small of my back and between my toes. Everyone mostly ignored me. I leaned forward and held my stomach and closed my eyes and hoped the ground would open up and swallow me and my baby because if Melissa didn't want us, I didn't want to do one more thing with my life. I don't know how long I sat there. The chatter died down as the next class period started. I had study hall or French, I couldn't even remember. The quiet was nice. I lay on my back and looked up and I remembered being in the back of Klaus's truck and how all I thought about was Melissa and how she was all I ever thought about and how I was never going to know what her mouth felt like, inside where no one could see, or what her body would feel like holding me down and I wanted those things. I wanted them so bad.

As I lay on the ground in the middle of the quad, I wasn't a high school girl anymore. I wasn't a mother. I was nothing but want and need, sharp and miserable. For the first time in my whole life I thought I could leave Winesburg, I could just run away, me and my baby whose daddy really had a red neck. I had to run away because I couldn't survive in a place where she hated me and acted like I wasn't there. That's when I opened my eyes and Melissa was staring down at me.

I knew Melissa loved me when she laid my head in her lap. "No more boys," she said. I nodded, and burst into tears. She kissed me, softly, then not so softly. She took down her hair and dried my tears.

Jacques Derrida Writes Postcards to Himself from a Diner in Winesburg, Indiana

I am not the first French writer to venture into the heart of the American interior. It was Tocqueville, an inspector of prisons, who became distracted by the American character, finding at its heart a stability for the time, crafted by an obsession with equality and its jettisoning of rank, title, primogeniture, and the other trappings of the aristocratic landed elites. Beneath such skins, in other words, were other words. Take this "sandwich" for instance. It is an amalgam of the "raw" and the "cooked." A sign for both the great leavened leveling flatness of the culture nurtured on a denuded glacial plain and its assertion of its –ness-ness (it is known as "John's [after the proprietor of the bistro] Awful, Awful," a diminution of "Awful Big, Awful Good"). It is considered here to hold the highest of rank in the hierarchy of "sandwiches," said to be "the sandwich's sandwich" in the same way one can be "a writer's writer." This is an application of democracy, after all, at once stratified, but also (in its "bunned" variant) equilateral in its expression of difference and conformity. "*Le pain*," the "bun," is the architectural "quotation" of the dome (the English "pan" a verbal and visual pun as well as the literally vexed convex(ed) structure of the bun's upper segment), the vaulted space that (pantheistically) arches over all uniformly and simultaneously. Elections are held for such sandwiches as I am told by the "waitress," and, here, in an enabling parasitic text attached to the menu, I discover that this particular "breaded" pork (tender)loin has (on several occasions) garnered the award as "best" in the "fair(s)" of several Midwestern states. Significant is that this meat puck be peened flat first to within an inch of its life, its footprint allowed to expand (before the application of its "breading" [that is to say the meat is sandwiched by its own dermis of adhesive dough before said sandwich is sandwiched by the aforementioned sandwiching conventionally yeasted bun]) beyond the edges of the circular boundaries of the "bun" and beyond (and in its continuous beatings and poundings [known locally as "tenderization"]) in all directions, expand into a slim smear, a skid of flesh, even beyond the limits (and this is crucial [in the sense of "crossed"]) of the ceramic "plate" or "platter" that frames the whole meat delivery device's delivery device. The massive flatness of the (tendered)loin is made even more evident by the rigorously induced rigor of the *deep* (emphasis mine) fat frying of the dead (though still elastic and recently stretched) flesh into the consistency of plied wood. The now encrusted cutlet is meant to expand (theoretically) horizontally beyond the surrounding event horizon of the plate and, eventually, the place. As I unhinge the "bun" in order to "dress" the sandwich with additional limpid veneers of a single lettuce leaf, a thinly sliced slice of pickle, a squeeze-bottled skim of yellow-washed paste of mustard, I realize that the compacted (tenacious)loin is a kind of mirror (mirrored), reflecting not me so much as the surface of "me" ("Derrida") or, even more exact, the (tentative)loin is a kind of anti-mirror mirror (mirror), not reflecting so much as absorbing light into the striations of its now heat-induced, chemically altered coatings, not a skin so much as the scrim that adheres to skin (a scum on the smooth surface of a pond that, in its flatness [both in the dimensional and optical calibrations], argues against even the concept of "depth"), a skin's skin skinned. The "sandwich" (itself) is constructed out of (empty) "words," ("empty") calories wrapped in the "whiteness" (the absence of color) of white bread. The "self" sandwiched as "sandwich." Not a "prison" of walls (walls) but of *floors* "sandwiched" together. The sign, "I," and the signifier for "I" (the "'I'") collapse—the serifed capital on the top pancaking upon the serif at the foot. The middle (stuffing) compressed (ground to grout), the whole thing reduced to a *line*, an *"under"line, under lined*, a line the thickness of this postal card, the depth of this stamp (the stamp's intaglio image [of an American author] made of etched and stippled *lines*), the slick spit of the lick of my tongue positioned between the *stamp* (as in "to press down") and the card with its inscribed (and inscription of) surface, of place, with its (future) postmark a tattoo (to be) absorbed into the (skimmed) skin.

Pete, Waste Lab Technician

Sometimes when late at night I think I see someone out of the corner of my eye, it is really only one of those roving shadows. They rove up on a wall or behind me when I am pushing an empty gurney into the Waste Lab. I do not know why it is called the Waste Lab.

I am really not afraid of anything.

When I was small, for a short time, buttons frightened me.

The gurneys have a peculiar smell, hard to describe.

I am not really sure what I should tell you about myself. The roving shadows are what come to mind because they are really so startling and mysterious, but there is also a cafeteria which at night is inhabited by a number of talkative zombies. They call themselves the Undead (predictably). And they jabber. Blah blah. They do not eat much, mainly the candy bars and juice boxes. I have discovered that they don't like meat, which seems strange to me.

Strictly speaking, I am not in charge of the Waste Lab. If you care to know what the Waste Lab looks like there are three boxy windows up very high which require a device with a hook for opening, beneath which there are the walls with all the gurneys pushed up against them. That leaves a space in the middle of the room which I enjoy traversing. The floor is golden, as is the entire floor of this building.

I have mentioned that those gurneys really stink.

It is odd that through the Waste Lab windows which are up very high the view is always the same—night or day, it is as if a sheet of white paper occupies the space outside each window so that one has the impression of glowing blankness, of there being no world at all on the other side of the windows of this building much less the world of Winesburg, Indiana, with its perfectly restored vintage fire engine, adult movie theater, and my mother's Gift Shoppe, to name three things cherished by me.

You might deduce that zombies have something to do with the roving shadows. But even zombies cannot be in two places at once. The zombies, as previously stated, are in the cafeteria—all twenty, I counted—and here right outside the Waste Lab are the usual crop of shadows doing their usual roving up and down the walls and stretching and shrinking along the golden floors as is their wont and occasionally folding into little envelope-sized packages or splitting in twos and veering off in different directions and snaking down opposite corridors.

Perhaps meat reminds the zombies of their own lost and mostly forgotten bodies. Their own disintegrating bodies which are kept at the Winesburg Wondrous Peace and Light Haven which is also a dog and cat burial ground.

I prefer the words "burial ground" to the word "cemetery."

One of the zombies, coincidentally, is called Pete also. He usually sits alone at one of the orange tables next to the kitchen door over by the window. In the cafeteria, the windows are filled with heavy black rectangles at this time of day. Once in a while one of the roving shadows streaks across and if you didn't know better you would think it was a tree.

More than once I have attempted to approach Pete for conversation. Of all the chattering zombies he is the quietest, but still he jabbers quietly to himself. They cannot help their jabbering; it is some kind of condition, probably, that they have to put up with as zombies.

Other than the gurneys there are large plastic barrels in the Waste Lab which they say are filled with eyes. Hard to believe, but I never checked. Though most things do not frighten me, I would not like to look into a barrel of eyes. Don't ask me why.

Pete jabbers mostly about physics. E equals em-cee squared type of thing. Archimedes's experiments with buoyancy; Isaac Newton and his various theories of gravity and planetary orbiting. Pete, I said to him once, do you think the elliptical orbiting of ideas is a *replica* of the elliptical orbiting of the planets? In other words, I said, still arguing with Pete, who was gazing into one of the thick black rectangles that occupy the cafeteria window frames and moving his lips very slowly, not chewing his Starburst but jabbering, could it be that we are ourselves *replica* universes and that, for example, Winesburg, Indiana, is a *replica* of the Milky Way so that, in conclusion, might we say that each of us is a *replica* of Winesburg, Indiana, and vice versa? Sometimes I blow my own mind.

The other zombies sit in clumps along the side wall away from the windows and near the machines. I have never seen an animal—dog or cat—zombie and I hope I do not.

My mother, who is no longer alive, did once own a business called the Gift Shoppe which is also no longer alive, so to speak, having been appropriated by a company whose team of grinning salespeople are always dressed in orange jackets. I have no idea what kind of business is conducted there. In my mother's day, gifts were sold. Now, who knows?

The waste room has fat white hoses coiled against the ceiling. Strange but true. I have often been tempted to ask Mr. M_____ the purpose of the hoses and why, of all places, they reside on the ceiling of the waste lab, but Mr. M_____ never seems inclined to converse. I only ever meet him when he is leaving the building and I am entering it and at these times he averts his eyes and hustles himself into a white Chevrolet.

I don't know how helpful this has been. I am who I am. The zombies come and go; they can be relied on to clean up after themselves—candy wrappers in the trash, chairs carefully replaced on top of tables. The roving shadows continue to mystify with their irrational movement, but I am accustomed to the Mysterious, it does not frighten me. I recently remarked to Pete that we are all enshrouded in mystery and walk around in its fog. Who is Mr. M_____ exactly and where does the white Chevrolet take him? What product is so important that six orange-jacketed salespeople must overtake a nice Gift Shoppe? What about those hoses in the waste lab? The smell of the gurneys? The zombies and their dislike of meat? All mysteries that, as far as I can tell, will never be satisfactorily explained.

Constance H. Wootin

Most people think that the old murals they see in old post offices were painted by out-of-work artists, hired by the WPA (if they can even recall that alphabet agency), during the Great Depression. Mere make-work for hard times, they think. That's not quite correct.

The Winesburg post office was a standard design for 1934, a scaled-down Greek temple on the outside with fluted columns and smooth limestone walls quarried in Bedford, Indiana, where you can see the quarrying of the blocks of Bedford limestone for the Winesburg PO depicted on the mural in the Bedford PO.

All those murals are in all those lobbies. Terrazzo floors. Walnut trim. The three walls not the wall with the front doors have the windows where the clerks work and the rest is bricked with the tarnished PO box doors. Each door is studded with combination locks, knobs that spin a pointer from letter to letter inscribed above the little glass window with the golden decaled number.

I was born in Winesburg in 1930. The first thing I remember is the lobby of the PO. My mother brought me to the lobby and showed me the picture on the stamp she bought. It was a picture of a woman sitting in a chair. The stamp was all pink, the image etched on the paper of the stamp in pink whorls. My mother told me the stamp pictured a painting of an artist's mother. She showed me how to lick the stamp. I remember her pink tongue behind the pink stamp licking its back. She showed me how to stick the stamp to the big white envelope. She let me lick another stamp she tore from a sheet of stamps. I tried to see my tongue lick the glue. The glue tasted like glue.

On the wall to the right of the mail slot Mother pushed the mail through was the massive scaffolding, the only thing in the brand new lobby not neat and orderly. It was rickety even then when it was new. It had been thrown together as the building was built, lattices and buttresses and cross-bucks and beams that made some room around the postmaster's door (it said so on the fogged glass and still does: POSTMASTER). There was a man up on top of the nest of the scaffolding, sitting on an egg that wasn't really an egg but a can of white paint. He was looking closely at the blank wall way up there.

The PO murals weren't make-work so much as advertisements. President Roosevelt wanted to signal to the towns and villages that the federal government would, from now on, have a new relationship with its citizens. Times had changed. The post office had been the only U.S. agency with which most people had any connection. So the new post offices were post offices for the people, for everyone. And the post offices would have stories to tell.

I am eighty years old. I have an electric lift that lifts me up to the top of the scaffolding. It is always warmer up here, right under the ceiling, and the sweet odor the plaster puts out as it evaporates seems to drape itself over, like laundry on a line, the fret work of cables and struts, turnbuckles and guy wires that support the paint-splattered platform. A real drapery of 6 mil Visqueen shapes the vapors, a thin atmosphere of thinner that has been circulating here for forever. No one below can see how the mural is going. It is in progress, has been in progress since 1934. The only post office mural in the Winesburg PO begun in the Great Depression is the only post office mural that has never been finished. While other murals are restored or are removed or discovered under coats of plaster that have been seared away by means of laser beams, this mural inhabits another state altogether, suspended. Suspended, as I am suspended floating on these persistent clouds of dank water and wet lime here in the lobby near the ceiling of the Winesburg PO.

The mural is a fresco mural so each day I apply a new wash of lime mortar and begin to paint, injecting the pigment in the drying plaster. As the wall sweats and squeezes out its moisture, I can feel the coolness glaze my cheek. I'm an old woman, nearly blind now. I am right on top of the painting even though I have several layers of loupes and lenses and magnifying glasses wired to my head. I lick the point of my brush to shape its point. I taste dirt in all its colors. I taste seaweed and the sea. I taste bones and shells. I taste iodine. I taste lead.

The man in my memory up on the scaffolding painting the wall, that was Bart Harz, the painter originally hired to tell the story of Winesburg in the PO's mural. The artists back then were encouraged to depict a historical moment in the murals, celebrate native crops or manufactured goods, capture a geographical feature, or highlight an ethnic or cultural peculiarity. Color the local color.

For years, as we stood in line, waiting to approach the clerk's window for service, we would look up at Bart, sitting on the platform near the ceiling, staring at the big empty wall. Or after mailing a letter, flipping the flap door a time or two to make sure the letter slid down the chute, we would turn and say to Bart, "How's it going, Bart?" Or dialing the combination of the boxes and sorting out the day's mail, we would ponder Bart pondering on his perch. It was hard to leave the lobby after a while. You wanted to linger just a moment more. And then a moment more. And then another moment to see if, right then, Bart would, at that moment, apply the first brushstroke. You didn't want to miss it. Or, at least, see him begin to sketch, trace out a gesture with a piece of charcoal. This went on for years.

There is plenty of paint on the wall in front of me now. There is too much paint. Layers and layers of it. I am constantly revising the faces in the fresco as the faces they are modeled on change and grow older. I must slather on a new skim coat each day. Each day draw the hairlines back a little farther on the men whose hairlines are receding. Or gray the hair on the ones whose hair is graying. Change the color of the hair on those who've changed the color of their hair. Redo the styles as the styles go in and out of fashion, document this haircut or that, and, every spring, get ready to coif the prom hairdos for that spring's junior girls at Durkheim High. And that's just the hair. There is the clothing to do. The glasses that have moved to bifocals, trifocals. Hats and gloves have mostly disappeared. The dollop of sparkle that represents an engagement ring, wedding ring, and then in some cases, painting over the rings. Shades of lipstick. The skin itself reflects the seasons—the summer's bronze tan, the lake effect's pale pale. I add the wrinkle here. The age spot there. A scar or two. I work hard to paint a patch of a palsy creeping over a face.

"How's it going, Constance?" I hear someone shout to me from below. I wave over my shoulder. It goes, I think, it goes.

During lunch, I sit on the platform dangling my feet out over the lobby. I peel back all of my optics, revealing my naked eyes. I watch the citizens of Winesburg below doing their postal business. Jim Hitch is going out of town. Charlie Kimble has a notice that there is something too big to fit in his box. Wanda Weintraub asks for a duck stamp. Omar B Wells (there is no period after the B) has a package to mail to his sister in Peoria. Johnson Jr. is filling out his selective service form. And Sallie Nadir is showing little Josh how to peel a stamp, the Liberty Bell, from the booklet she just bought and apply it to a letter his mother then slides in the slot. Josh looks back up to me looking down at him. He sticks out his tongue. I stick out mine.

Bart never painted a lick of paint. Ever since Mother showed me the picture of the painting of a mother on that stamp, I have wanted to be an artist. When Mother realized that, she took me back to the PO and asked Bart to give me lessons in drawing, painting, composition when he took breaks from his not-working work. He needed the money, he said, and he needed the break from the break that, up until he started teaching me, looked pretty much like what he was doing when not on break. I sat on an up-ended unopened paint can in the middle of the PO's lobby and sketched Bart as he worked or, more accurately, as he didn't work. Charcoal and pastels, washes and inks, pencil and pen and brush, watercolors, oils. I even did a pointillistic collage out of pictures I snipped from Life magazine, now dead. He'd have me help him rebuild his scaffold. I would re-rig the poles and platforms, the struts and the netting. The airy scrim that hung from the ceiling like a cloud. I would sketch Bart and the scaffold and the PO boxes and the empty wall, the white whiteness of it stretching on and on behind him.

All those studies prepared me to fill in for Bart Harz after he bit the dust after the war. The commission came to me, a codicil to his will. I was bequeathed the rigging and the rigmarole in rigor mortis all those years. The dried-up paint, all those shades of blue, the thinners and the pigments, the dry points and the abandoned stencils, the masking tape and the spent snap lines. I was willed the pots and kidney-shaped French palettes with their histories of miscalculated mixing, rainbows of mud and dung derivations, and the wall, I inherited the empty wall and its fifteen years of priming, priming, priming, priming.

That wall is filled with faces now, a portrait of everyone in town, and each of those faces I touch up each day, age them and gray them, add the wide-eyed new arrivals and close the eyes of the citizens who have died, as if a camera has caught them blinking in the sun, not sleeping for eternity. It is a field in which the populace of Winesburg is arrayed and the field has depth of field and the folks in the further back ranks shrink in that illusion of distance, dwindle to the distant vanishing point. Some face no bigger than this "o" here, and with my skill of chiaroscuro and a triple aught brush I contour even that minute visage with the expressions of joy and wonder.

They are all looking up. They are looking up to Bart on his jury-rigged tower, his back to the PO lobby below. It is all trompe l'oeil, and Bart is bent to his work painting the people of Winesburg spread out before him in attitudes of joy and wonder looking back at the artist who is rendering them so effortlessly and with such detail.

And there, there I am on my paint can stool, an egg, looking over Bart's soft cotton shoulder. I am in profile, depicted as some antique muse, attempting to sketch the artist's, Bart's, own profile I alone can see. It seems I am whispering into his ear, a flash of a pearl pink tongue, a kind of spark between the synapses, rendered between my lips. Still wet, the image glistens. I dismantle all my lenses and glasses and goggles. I lean into this point of paint, the picture closing in on me. And with my own tongue, I tongue the image of my tongue, taste it, that metal taste, that taste of earth, that taste of pink. And with my tongue I draw out the tongue-shaped image of my tongue in the fresco. Shape it. Give it depth and texture. I lap and flick. I am blind to it. It is all by feel. This final touch. This articulation. This accent. This annunciation.

But I myself, I will leave unfinished. A kind of spirit, a ghost. I am an impression, impasto. A blur really. A bunch of hasty gestures, smudged lines, and smeared paints in unsubtle hues. I float like a cloud, undone, my gossamer gown's draping all hurried and fudged, naive, here all flat, stiff, matte. My face, except for around the mouth, a blank, traced, an empty outline, still waiting to be finished, sealed, fixed, done after all these years, done. Finally finished after I have completed all of my studies of this little precinct of this unending, this infinite, heaven.

Dear Class of 2011

Dear Class of 2011,

The room as I sit looking at it (once again) is the usual square-and-rectangle composite, only now it contains an additional rectangular item: this handheld reading device for which I thank you, though it will not stave off loneliness, if that's what you were thinking. At this point I don't even care anymore. It's fine, let it be there, loneliness, I like it. In fact I'm so used to it, I prefer it that way because then I can do things exactly as I think they should be, exactly as I want them.

I have all my news stories lined up on my new handheld reading device, hundreds of them, and I'll read them in the order I think is best. For the next two years I will be slowly catching up on my news story reading. Two years from now, while you are home for the holidays, come check in on me and I assure you I will be almost caught up on my news stories, all my favorite columnists, all the little tips for daily living and pieces of nutritional advice that you know I've been waiting for, my favorite stories about the White House, what one government said about another. I will have read them all and have a solid schedule for reading future ones. If I'm busy one week, I'll have to hurry home and catch up on my news story reading because one can get far behind with these handheld things and you know the pain, the sense of a lack of completion one feels when one has to delete a bunch of news stories unread—not that you missed something important (though you may have, who knows), but that you didn't complete the series. (Where does that need come from? I don't know.) Now that I have this new handheld reading device I can plan away and download furiously, every tip and news bit and update, get them all on this thing before it's too late and they vanish, before the internet space hatch closes over them and they are gone. What will happen if they do vanish? Nothing, of course! Who cares. It will be simply another incomplete project like all the others. Who cares. I never finished *Ulysses* (who cares). I didn't clean out the car (who cares). I don't know how to love (who cares). I'm alone in this room (who cares). My only baby died (who cares). My brother's in a wheelchair (who cares). The sky glows (who cares). I never figured out what I wanted (who cares). I still have years to go (who cares). I can hear sounds outside—school buses, voices, rain (who cares). This minute will never end (who cares).

Yours,

Emily Walls
Emile Durkheim High School English

Walt "Helper" Voltz

You are looking at the proud owner of the shortest short line in the United States or really what you are looking at is the longest story about the shortest short line in the country.

Your eyes go back and forth over these lines like my engine shuttles back and forth on my siding. My railroad runs 5,284 feet east to west, west to east. I have 150-pound flat-bottomed rail, and every morning I don my gandy dancer's hard hat and walk the length of the property, checking the joint plates and lag bolts, the tie plates and spikes, the ties themselves with their date nails I have stamped and installed. The ballast is pristine ballast, crushed quartz (from the smallest quarry in the United States, a scooped-out glacial moraine banking up against the property) that sparkles in the Indiana sunlight. I switch the switches on either end of the line that connect me to the mainline of the Chicago, Fort Wayne and Eastern, née the old Conrail, née the older Pennsylvania, née the older still Pittsburgh, Fort Wayne and Chicago. I check the switch points and the frogs. I maintain what's left, hereabouts, of the telegraph too. I have a shed at each terminus of my line. I will send train orders from one depot to the other, following the old rules of the old rulebooks, about train movements, labor practices, and traffic. I've been told I have a distinctive hand on the key. Dah dah, dit, dah dah dah.

My motive power? I roster one engine, a GP7 "Geep," numbered "4." Rolling stock? One boxcar serving my one customer, the Marcel Box Company. A hopper to haul my ballast. One mixed baggage and parlor car. And I have one crummy, a caboose you call it, or clown wagon, hack, waycar, doghouse, go-cart, glory wagon, monkey wagon, brain box, palace, buggy, van, cabin, or cab—a train of names naming that car. It's a steeple type, the crummy, extended vision, with cupola and bay windows, which serves both as corporate headquarters and my home.

My livery's a deep, deep-sea blue, almost black, and I apply my own spray paint graffiti at night so that during the day I can stay busy erasing the make-believe vandalism. Folks bumping over the crossing up the way can see me and imagine my diligence in maintaining the fleet. I walk the track, check for messages, and fire up the Geep for the daily run a mile up the track, a layover there for lunch, and, then, a reverse move back down the line.

The road is known as the Winesburg & Winesburg, reporting as WW, but the name's not accurate. My right-of-way lies right outside the corporate limit of the namesake town, in a whole other town, named Helper. Helper, Indiana. Here is the story on that. In days gone by, the mighty Pennsylvania Railroad ran over three hundred trains a day along this adjacent route, calling it the Broadway. Broadway because from Chicago to New York the road was, at least, four standard gauge tracks wide. That way, the streamlined passenger limiteds could coast along the inside rails while the heavy freights and locals jostled on the outside ones. Not a train idling, waiting for a meet or juggling an overtake. I was a boy then, and I remember the endless pulse of it. Numbered and named trains so long they broke them into sections that sped like dots and dashes on the wire, one after another, separated only by a minute or two, tail end to head end, as they clocked east, clocked west, the specials flying white flags at their smokeboxes, the red lights beating a slow pulse beating it out of town. So many, the four tracks solid with riveted iron, quilted steel, pleated aluminum, varnished wood, a rapid rapid hustling east, shuffling west. All gone now. The road demoted to tertiary line. A unit train or two, toting Wyoming coal to a power plant, power by from time to time and then roar back the other way with the hoppers and gondolas all empty empty. Full of nothing now.

From here east to Fort Wayne there is a steady upward grade. Fort Wayne is known as the Summit City after all, 765 feet above sea level, high point on the line. I started on the Pennsy firing the K-4s on that grade. The Pacifics were wholly underpowered to haul all the tonnage, so, often, the company double-headed or triple-headed a train. A little past Winesburg, you could feel the steam's pressure bleed out the boiler, the smoke belched and bleached, the driving wheels slipping even as the engineer sanded and scolded me to lay on more coal. It was like that children's book about the engine that would think, I think, I think I can, the huffing and the sliding in the cylinders, matching up with the beat of the repeating words. I think I can, I think I can, you know the one. But all the thinking in the world could not outthink the physics of centripetal force. I dropped right down out of the cab and left the engineer in the lurch, licking my backside with his cursing as he hove to and stoked his own firebox. I outwalked the train into town. I think I can, I think I can, indeed.

It was back then that the Company, in its wisdom, built the little switchyard hereabouts and stocked it with a string of "helper" engines that coupled on the tail ends of the stalling trains as they leaned into their climbs, and pushed them up the long grade to Fort Wayne, a steady acceleration, a long reach.

That was me in the cab of the Geep (the Geep, then, painted in Brunswick Green, the stenciled "Pennsylvania" in that buff yellow foil) running cab forward on the tail end of a mixed freight drag out of Chicago, waving to the kids of Winesburg, who matched the train's slow pace with a sloppy jog or standing on the pedals of their Huffys, all the time yanking their arms up and down, a pantomime for me to toggle the horn switch which I did at the crossing, a tootle here and there, the smoke standing up from the vent of the exhaust as my little engine dug into the track, the slack, the brakes hissing and wheels slipping, just a little bit, the sun catching the glaze of the window on the cupola of the crummy just ahead, and through the glare I saw the red-bandanaed neck of the conductor there, sitting on his perch thinking through the manifest of all the cargo in the cars stretching out ahead in his head. Long drag freight moves like that contained most anything back then—automotive parts, sheet steel, appliances, tires, coiled wires, artificial flowers, rolls of newsprint, bolts of cloth, ingots, springs, tin toys, T-shirts, boiled ham, chlorine gas, pallets of lumber, screws, sawdust, sail canvas, fuses, ballast, turpentine, crates of light bulbs, live cattle, mattresses, bone meal, popcorn, potash, cans, drums, and boxcars and boxcars containing boxes and boxes of boxes. And more cars, deadheading empty, containing nothing, the hollow booming of the empty empty empty empty cars on the way to some faraway siding, some yard, some depot someplace somewhere.

I would hitch a ride back the other way, back down the hill listing from Fort Wayne, attaching my idling locomotive to the tail end of the westbound mixed freight, the Geep's pneumatic lines slaved to the big road engines' dynamic brakes up front. I was a drag on the drag. Dead weight. Deadheading myself now as if an empty. Doing nothing. Taking in the view of corduroyed fields, the smudged wood lots, awkward windmills, the brittle barns and fermenting silos, the outbreaks of little Indiana towns—Larwil, Arcola, Atwood and Inwood, Log Cabin. My Geep's job now to tap the forward momentum of the cascading tare and tonnage spilling down the slope. No runaways. The deadman switches all depressed. You know the deadman switch, yes? The metal pedal that needs to be tread on steady in order for the train to run. If the engineer falls asleep or, heaven forefend, keels over dead, that switch comes unengaged, the whole train sent into emergency, grinds and grinds to a dead stop. A precaution, that switch.

And there I was, a brake on the back end of all those trains now, nursing the weight of all of it with an easy drifting coasting, coasting down into the pleasant seat of Winesburg, its orderly grid of streets queuing up into long strings of little neat boxes with the smoke from all those chimneys puffing like antique engines in a hostler's yard.

The conductor, then, comes out onto the platform between his crummy and the Geep's pilot, gives me a little wave as he springs the hoses free and knocks the knuckle coupler loose, scrambles up from his knees as the train pulls away barreling west. I am left behind. To drift. I skate into town. All inertia. All tendency. I'm powered down. The highballing train speeds off, the block signals tripping red, red, red in its wake.

I did this flying drop so many times, I had it all timed out to perfection. I would run out of steam on a dime. My little engine, its bell ringing, slowing, slowed to a stop just shy of my turnout, stopped, stopping its brakes all seized. I'd hop down, then, to throw my switch, then, clamber onboard to start her up and nudge the throttle just enough to ease the now panting engine home.

That's my story, then. Back then. My story now is that daily routine I have already laid out. Each day, I move my little train from one end of the siding to the other. I push the empty boxcar to the loading dock of the box factory and set it out there, backing away back up the line, moving the remaining three-car consist back to the other end of the line. I will send a telegram or two to be picked up by myself on the other end of the line when I get back there. Mostly train orders and such. Then Burt will come over from the plant to tell me the car's been loaded up and locked, and I chuff down there to couple on and push the load to the far switch where in a day or two the road engine of the Chicago, Fort Wayne and Eastern will pick it up. I leave it there and retreat up the line and go about my business until the empty boxcar returns. My business then is just moving the train back and forth on the 150-pound rails, making sure the rails don't rust, until I have to fetch the empty off the main line in a day or two and start the logistics up all over again.

So, will that do you? All your questions answered? Is that enough human interest, this old man and his little train? Train lines and railroads are abandoned every day now. Mile after mile. You see the rusting rails, the ties turning to dust, ballast washed away. A depressing depression where a grade once cut through a hillock. The rights-of-way, if they are lucky, get turned into hiking trails or bike paths, or banked until the day we might need the easement again to get us from where we are to where we need to go.

That? Oh, that? That siding siding off my siding? My own abandonment. That is the old necropolis branch. You can barely make it out. The ditch weed, the paw-paw, and the sassafras saplings reclaiming it, disappearing in the undergrowth, the overhang, the general moss and vine. I should schedule a special maintenance-of-way train back into that slough and clear it out with paraquat, pickax, and chainsaws. There was the time, when that branch was clear, I'd make a run or two down that line every day, bringing my cargo to its last offloading. That branch meanders for a mile or two and then doubles back through Throw Park and the Waterworks to the platform, now decaying, at the Wine Dark Sea Cemetery and Crematoria.

Those were the days! The caskets, in state, on the catafalques I built myself, rested in the parlor of the parlor car, the mourners and the undertaker's men from Jonesing Funereal Funerals arrayed in the upholstered banquettes built in beneath the big venetian-blinded windows. The mounds of flowers off-gassing that waxy scent of flowers on the edge of rot. The pace was slow through the woods, the glades, over the one through truss bridge, its girders painted lamp black, the color the Pennsy used to call "boxcar color." I wore my dress bib overalls of dark blue denim, a black plume in my engineer's shako, and I wailed with the air horn, its harmonic bawling ricocheting off of the draping leaves of the weeping willows in Shaw's weeping willow nursery, a dirge accompanied by the cottonwood and sycamore along the south fork of the Fork River. I blasted a blast of the horn as if the sound alone would keep the tracks cleared of creepy ever-creeping vegetation. I crept along, a mournful pace, the joints in the rail not click-clacking so much as the stuttered thumping of a muffled drum beat, punctuating the thrum of the Geep's prime mover that spewed ozone in the air, throwing off from the spinning magnets in its overheated core.

I pause today in the silence of my telegraph shack for that line to come alive again. Oh, to field orders from the Jonesing undertakers again, to decode that black framed message once more. A transshipment inbound, perishable goods to be expedited. That dah dah dah, dit dit dit, dah dah dah. But I could wait forever it seems. Bodies move through space by other means of transport now. More efficient for sure but less impressive, less illustrative. There is something about a locomotive moving through the landscape, something so big, even my little engine here, all that metal, that power, that sound, connected to earth through this tiny tangent, a kiss of steel on steel, no bigger than a dime.

That reminds me of the kids who still come down to my line and put the pennies on the rails to watch the change change before their eyes, the slugs turned into holy wafers by the slow rolling of this hulking shadow I pilot through time and space.

There is an uphill grade that leads to the terminus in the cemetery. It is steep. The manifest slows to a crawl. I think I can. I think I can. You remember. I remember firing the boilers on those old Pacifics. My helping all those freight trains down the line. I keep my foot pressed down on the deadman pedal on my Geep. The horn warbles and howls. The mourning passengers, the ambulatory ones, dismount and latch on to the enameled handholds and bronze handrails on the outside of the midnight blue parlor car, lightening the load but also putting a few extra foot-pounds into the tractive effort of the train. I think I can. I think I can. I lean forward in the cab. Lean on the horn. The bell peals and reports. The platform hoves to. The whistle shrieks and sighs. I put all my weight on the deadman as if it is an accelerator and the race has just begun.

Frances Parker

I have been a doctor in this town for many years now. You won't find me in the phone book, but if you go past the sign for Chief Raintree's Village and the llama farm by the trailer sale lot and then take that winding road, which can be foggy at night and deceptive, you will come to an abandoned church—not abandoned anymore, that is. My dogs will be out front but don't let them scare you. My friend Ansel is the pharmacist I use, the one at the drugstore on the square downtown that still has the real chocolate malts. He measures out the pills right in front of you. He's also the one who's been remodeling that big three-story house perched on a hill above Ash Street for about ten years now. They had that St. Bernard tied up by the garage for a while and a truck parked out front that had "Barely Gettin' By" written on the side. You might have seen it. The front yard is a profusion of flowers this summer—lilies, daisies, bergamot—and the siding is halfway up. A nice slate color. But the brick sidewalk in front is still all torn up. It's just a few houses up from the homeless shelter. Sharon, my partner, always says, would you trust a pharmacist who has started over so many times on his house and still can't get it right? And I say, would you trust a doctor who lives in an abandoned church full of unpacked boxes and musical instruments and paintings and who still isn't moved in? Barely gettin' by, Sharon, barely gettin' by. That's my motto. My father was a luthier by trade—he made violins and cellos. He believed that if you shone a red light on an instrument, it would sound different than if you shone a blue light on it, that color and sound were somehow connected. He conducted all sorts of experiments with wood. He was always trying to discover the secret of Stradivarius, cooking amber in the front yard, mixing vermillion with rosematter, simmering the wood over a fire for months on end. He believed that if he could just discover the secret, he would be a rich man. I used to love the fact that he believed there was a secret—that was the thing I admired most about him—that he never gave up trying to find it. But I don't really think there is a secret. Red light, blue light, if you tell someone that a violin is a Stradivarius it will sound good to them. My father would spend hours walking around with a violin in his hand, tapping, tapping the wood, then listening, his head cocked to one side. What was he listening for? I always start by leading the patient through what used to be the sanctuary when this was a church, past the one or two old church pews stacked with books and drums and gongs, past what used to be the altar, now with a tapestry of Jesus hanging there, because why not? he was a good man, and into the healing room, where I listen, carefully, until I hear the sound of his heart. I listen for a good long while.

Emmalene's Bakery and Bait Shop

Catman's truck eases past the gleaming shop window, the boat trailing behind like a ghost in the cautious, blue night. A blip and it's gone. Like a heart monitor. Like a nocturnal creature out on the chase.

It's my imagination, maybe, but this early in the morning anything can happen.

Sometimes, in the middle of this middle ground before the sun rises, a feeling washes over me that I *am* this town. There's nothing between. It encompasses me. I am irreparable. I am exquisite. Salt. Yeast. Sugar. Worms. Hand-tied flies. That's my shop: Emmalene's Bakery and Bait.

Have some food is what I say. Catch some fish.

This week I walk the streets to work in the wee hours. My car broke down and Allison Transmission's taking me to the cleaners. I think about me and Winesburg, Indiana—the two of us like lovers who've quarreled too much. My shoes tap-tap-tap on the asphalt.

The Dairymart glows green like a Bible. The Dollar General is closed shut like a map. The Hot Spot buzzes its neon: a crazy blue cowboy loop, loop, looping his lasso out front. The girls wear shorts with heels now, I notice. Guys have these jeans down low. The bar thump, thumps. Everyone's still drinking beer though.

As I stroll past, my own form of invisible, I hear the distinct clack-clack of pool balls as they break and scatter. Smokers huddle by the front door where lanky weeds sprout up along the cracked sidewalk.

These days when I'm out and about I keep to the periphery, slide into doorways. I stay unseen so I can remain a wily observer. In the past I was down in there, part of Winesburg's middle. But I'm over all that.

Jamie comes to mind as I turn the corner near the bridge, wait for a semi truck to roll by spouting diesel exhaust before I can cross. Still makes me hum to think about him. Down there by the river, the two of us. Down in parts of each other all the time. Groaning like the machine we were, those days. We sputtered and spilled ourselves out like most young lovers do. Picking at the seams while we tried to stitch something together.

That passion for tracking down and cuddling with the dark and unknown wanes within me each year. Now, I just like to know what I know. It's enough. But a few weeks ago I Googled Jamie to see if I could find him out there in the world. Blank, blank, blank, said the blinking cursor.

But not knowing him now helps me keep things straight— from now to then. I can't add anything. The times with Jamie exist up to the point when I can't remember anymore. And that's all right.

As I walk through the sneaking-in fog, I think about how if maybe I opened my mouth wide the town itself could crawl in and take up all the space it's yet to have. I'd just let it. That's how I feel, and I know it's a little off. Like my car, nearly done for, waiting out there on the hill at Allison Transmission. My big beautiful Buick, bathed in moonlight like last rites. Loyal like a dog.

Walking to work, past the Hot Spot and its thumping thump, down into the little part of town that looks like a town—down the side streets by myself, I put my arms out straight and open my mouth wide. Waiting.

It feels good.

Jamie loved me, I'm sure of that. What I did back to him I'm not certain. Back then when I didn't slump around thinking big thoughts, I felt a kind of feral compunction. I needed to move around inside and outside everything at once. Jamie just sat still and beautiful on his front porch with the wildflowers popping up here and there, announcing what was what. Jamie all droopy cigarette and muscled arms. All flannel shirt and boots. Jamie with a perfect smile. Humming. He scratched his head, right above his left ear, and he said, "Emmalene, all I know is I love you. I can't help it." Then he looked out over me to the flat, flat skyline. He squinted like he wished he could erase it all, including me, knowing though that he couldn't, which I thanked God for.

I remember feeling strong and right. I remember smiling, basking in the kind of love he had for me. I remember a rumbling bumblebee nudging each and every flower in sight just once. I remember nudging Jamie's boot, holding his hand. I remember looking good but feeling like trouble. And I couldn't finish that story. I couldn't give it the ending he wanted. I needed to know he was there for me, and I needed to know I could do what I wanted.

Eventually I scratched at the screen to his basement bedroom window. He let me in. And there in that cozy light, standing beside his bed, I wrapped my arms around his neck and told him it was over. He didn't believe me, even though I told him by tomorrow

I would be off with someone else, Frank or Paul or Catman himself—can't remember which one came next. Jamie and I swayed then, there, to the soft music he had playing on his cassette player. I hummed into his neck for a while. I looked him right in the eye, pretending to be brave, watching his heart break.

He asked, "Will I ever see you again, Emmalene?"

It was the meanest thing I've ever done. With his arms hanging empty, my answer was never. Never. But I didn't say that.

My bakery is a blink on a side street. Some people forget about me for months but then they crave a butterscotch muffin and know where to come. Or maybe they want to take the kids fishing. They know. I tie flies while the bread rises soft and firm, like a sleeping pillow.

Tonight, I creak open the door. Step inside. I get hit full-on with that earthy-yeasty smell. Worms and bread. That scent travels with me wherever I go. I stumble here alone each morning to renew it, to sink inside this place I call home. I brew coffee, start in on mixing and waiting and tying. The steam rises up from my cup like a notion as Catman's ghost of a pickup sails on by.

Howard Garfield, Balladeer

My troubles began when I was ten and my parents spent the summer traveling, leaving me with my great-aunt in her decrepit gray Prairie School castle way out past the fairgrounds. This disconcertingly spry and moody octogenarian had a large collection of vinyl records, and out of desperate boredom one rainy afternoon, I took one at random, impaled it on the nub of her old Garrard SP25, and dropped the needle. A honeyed voice came pouring out of the speakers, crooning about a lumberjack drowned while freeing a logjam. It was Glenn Yarbrough, and I was lost.

It was music from a different era: the Weavers, the Limeliters, the New Lost City Ramblers, the New Christy Minstrels, the Brothers Four, the Stanley Brothers, the Carter Family, Richard Dyer Bennett, Eric von Schmidt, Dave Van Ronk, Buffy Sainte-Marie, the Kingston Trio, the Chad Mitchell Trio, the Clancy Brothers and Tommy Makem, Sonny Terry and Brownie McGhee, Blind Blake, Blind Willie Johnson, Blind Willie McTell, Blind Boy Fuller, the Blind Boys of Alabama, and many others. Probably she did not have all those records. It is partly my own present collection I must be thinking of.

I fell in love with those voices, singing gloriously on pitch and in harmony. They sounded bold and manly. I wanted to be like that—to sing sea chanteys, murder ballads, love ballads, work songs, protest songs, rebel songs, songs of the frontier, union anthems, Celtic dirges, Mississippi field hollers, Appalachian hymns, Oklahoma war whoops, Cape Breton lullabies, and satirical topical political ditties. This was the life for me—I would make my fortune as a folk singer. Naturally, I would find some like-minded fellows, and we would travel and have adventures together as balladeers. If I craved love, my heartfelt interpretation of "Poor Wayfaring Stranger" would win the heart of any woman I desired.

But these things never happened.

Through years of enthusiastic practice, first in my cellar and later at the Fort Wayne Academy of Music, I developed my voice until it was unquestionably powerful. But when I sang in public, I discovered that my voice did not have a thrilling and seductive effect on my listeners. To judge by their facial expressions, the principal emotion I elicited was puzzlement. But was this a condemnation of my singing, or merely unfamiliarity with my musical genre of choice? So far as I could tell, I was Winesburg's lone folk enthusiast, let alone folk singer. Perhaps my auditors' confusion only revealed their ignorance and limitation. Sadly, I lacked even a single aficionado to offer a trustworthy judgment.

My teachers at Fort Wayne praised my hard work, but did not offer me the introductions to the musical impresarios of Indianapolis that they gave to other students, so I returned to Winesburg and have been trying to make a go of it here for the last twenty years.

I teach music appreciation at the Richard Corey Technical Institute. It is an elective class. Not many students elect it. The metal lathe shop is next door to the room in which I teach. When

I play records, it is often difficult for my students to appreciate music properly because of the loud sound of metal being lathed.

Christmas Eve this year, I went to the annual family gathering of Patches, Garfields, and Studemonts at the big Patch house on Ash Street. Because I am unmarried and have no children, and am no longer youthful, I was there in a role I do not like, that of the funny uncle. "Why don't you boys play a game with your funny uncle Howard?" Julia Patch or Annie Studemont will say when they want to drink old fashioneds and flirt with the clergy.

That night, after many tumblers of bourbon, brandy, and hard cider had been passed around, Selma Patch made everyone gather at the Christmas tree so we could hear her six-year-old daughter sing. Brittany Patch was, as my students would say, a hot mess: teased blonde hair in a red and green felt elf costume, thirsty for attention, and arrogantly confident she could command it. She sang "O Holy Night" a cappella, belting it aggressively, without any sense of dynamics or nuance, or, for that matter, the most basic understanding of the lyrics. When she sang "The stars are brightly shining," it sounded as if "starzar" were one word. Nevertheless, because her voice had a kind of juvenile cuteness and clarity, there was an explosion of clapping and cheering, and calls for her to sing it again, which she did.

My ears pounded and my white Aran Islands sweater grew smotheringly hot. Toys and electronic gadgets littered the floor amidst torn wrapping paper. If had known for sure that an individual Barbie or PlayStation had been Brittany's, I would have crushed it under the heel of my worn, saddle-soaped cowboy boots. Instead, I excused myself, telling people that I was coming down with something, which in a sense I was.

In my Prius, I raced dangerously through the streets, splashing slush on the walks, tearing past all the Lutheran versions of holiday extravagance—the raw wood crèches, the plain white lights outlining the front hedge, the undecorated wreaths, the daring, almost Catholic blue lights under the eaves and around the windows—mentally shaking my fist at all humanity, until I got tired of it and drove over to Biff's Bar and Grill down by the railroad tracks.

Biff's was serving one other customer, a short wiry old fellow in dark blue denim bib overalls, his tan Carhartt jacket draped over the stool next to him, a hard hat on top of it. We were both drinking Hamm's, which seemed reason enough to strike up a conversation. He introduced himself as Walt, and said he worked on the railroad. After I'd bought a couple of rounds, he began to talk a blue streak about couplings, sidings, crummys, frogs, points, tie plates, grades, and lag bolts. He used his hands a lot as he spoke, showing me the way a knuckle coupling fit, or how a shunt worked. His hands were hard and red, with thick yellowing pads of callous on the flats of his palms, and ridges of gray callous along the edges of his crooked fingers, even up to the quick of his short blunt flat fingernails. Watching those hands, it occurred to me that I'd stumbled onto someone who was actual folk, maybe the only genuine folk person in Winesburg. My students were hardly folk, nor were the other teachers, or my relatives. Brittany Patch was probably the perfect mathematical inverse of folk. But this guy was unquestionably, unarguably unmitigated folk, and it felt like I'd been searching for him my whole life without knowing it.

By the time Biff kicked us out, we'd had more than a few, and it had turned Christmas. We stood there, beer-sodden in the raw foggy moistness of the new global-warming Midwest winter, not knowing what to do. "I think I'm going to walk my line," Walt announced. He settled his hard hat firmly with both hands, and headed down the slope toward the railroad track. After a moment, I followed him, a helpless, shambling schoolboy to his diminutive Pied Piper.

He'd perfected a kind of rolling trot that put his feet naturally on one tie after another. I tried to imitate it to keep pace behind him, but I kept hitching my gait, stepping on the gravel and tripping on the tie. A half moon the color of dirty milk blinked at us from between the low fast-moving clouds and shone on the silver rails, making them glint intermittently in a slow, hopeless SOS for the world itself. We said nothing, for nothing needed to be said.

Then came what I took ever so briefly to be a Christmas miracle. Walt began to hum a tune, one I knew well. It was "On the Banks of the Ohio." After passing through it once, he began to sing the first verse softly, as if afraid to disturb the delicate atmosphere he'd created with his humming. I understood him completely: the moonlight, the tracks, Christmas Eve with a stranger, it all cried out with an unspeakable sadness. His folkish heart, like mine, instinctively craved the melancholy relief that only a murder ballad could provide. I held my breath, not wanting to spoil things, until he came to the chorus and I joined in, quietly harmonizing a third above him on, "And only say that you'll be mine." He glanced at me, surprised, I thought, that I was privy to the signs and countersigns of his tribe. I started in on the second verse, and for a moment, we sang in a tempered, restrained unison. Then I couldn't help myself. I had a song to sing, and I was going to sing it all over this land. I let my voice swell to its fullest until it resonated in the natural echo chamber of the high dark embankments on either side of us. I charged into the chorus again, and then into the third verse, and "Willie dear, don't murder me." Then I realized he'd stopped singing, stopped trotting, and stood silently staring at me. On his face was the unmistakable expression of pure puzzlement.

Then he smiled a gentle, terrible smile, the kind you give your sick dog just before you put him to sleep. He patted me on the shoulder. "Thanks for the beers," he said. "You'll be okay. Sure you will." And with that, he turned and walked away. The moon was smothered in cloud for a long moment, and when it shone again, he had disappeared. He must have taken some secret railroad way known only to him.

I'd gotten my answer, one I couldn't deny or ignore. Of all the people in Winesburg, or Indiana, or the world, he was the one whose appreciation might have redeemed me, and I had seen plainly in his face that he preferred to let the earth and the mists swallow him whole rather than listen to one more bar of my grotesque singing. There in the dank, frigid shadows, on the tracks behind the back wall of the Business Athenaeum, its painted diploma and mortarboard blazoned as if to mark the exact spot of this graduation from my vainglorious dreams of becoming the thing I loved, I felt death inside me and knew that nothing would ever be the same.

Lost in despair, several sheets to the wind, I could have missed the rattle and hum of the rails, the trembling in the ground, the subtle but ominous change of pressure in the air, until it was too late. But I had enough presence of mind to look up as the single eye of light emerged from around a bend, rushing at me with murderous speed—an express freight on an inside through track. I jumped from the ties into the gravel culvert. A moment later the locomotive passed with a buffet of air that almost shoved me off my feet, and a piercing scream of steel wheel against steel rail, like a thousand metal lathes. I yelled in surprise and fear, but could not hear my own voice over the rattling cacophony, could not even feel it vibrate in my throat. I fell on my knees, threw my head back, and sang the last verse, about killing the only woman I loved because she would not be my bride—sang it unheard by any human ear, including my own, without any art or technique, forgetting everything I'd ever learned, sang only for the sake of singing. The train was long, the black hulks of the boxcars roared past me endlessly, as I sang to them beneath that lonely moonlit Athenaeum, sang to them of my despair, my longing, and my failure. When the train finally passed, I was left in the darkness, silent, trembling, and shaken, and I realized that only then could I even begin to think of myself as a folk singer.

Beau Morrow

"Blood is in our blood, son," my father used to say. He was the real butcher. I'm just a man who sells meat. He worked in the slaughterhouse at the north edge of town like his father before him and his father before him and his mother before him. My great-great-grandmother, Lil. The way they told it, she was the sweetest girl ever raised until her young husband was gored to death by a crazed, escaped bull. And after that she was a snake. A picture of her hung on our kitchen wall when I was growing up, right between the crucifix and the clock. A tiny woman in a long black dress, a veil over her face, standing right up against a hanging side of beef. When I was little, I thought her hands were soaked in blood but at some point I figured out that was gloves. Then I decided she probably wore them to cover up the blood. I hated to look at her and I looked at her at every chance I got. "You can't fight your fate," my father would say.

The fact is, I tried to as hard as I could. Genes or not, I knew I was no killer. I pretended to myself that the milkman was my father and that milk ran in my veins, white, bloodless blood. I understood it was weak, but when I dreamed of cows, their udders were full and my hands were on their teats. I could hear the tinny, rhythmic squirt into my pail. I patted them on their rumps when I was through—like a friend. And I knew it would just about kill my father if he found out. It took me to the day I graduated school and was scheduled to go to the slaughterhouse the next morning, the 5 AM shift, to tell him I wanted to own a dairy farm one day. An hour later he was dead. A heart attack. From shock.

I understood then that I could never fully leave the world of meat. I started at Karl's Finer Food the day after the funeral. But calling yourself a butcher when you've never butchered anything, just displayed it all prettied up with parsley sprigs and Easter basket plastic grass, is like calling yourself a musician because you can work your car radio. It's the kind of dishonesty that eats at your soul. And maybe my whole life has been about finding the one person alive who could understand that. Delia Barrymore, the podiatrist's wife. She was peering down into the sweating meat case one steaming summer afternoon, a kid or two hanging off each arm, when she said, "If you don't actually kill the animals yourself, are you truly a butcher? Aren't you more accurately a species of meat salesman?" And she looked right at me with green-blue eyes which are as close to circles as any eyes can be, and right when I realized they were the most beautiful eyes I'd ever seen, her children all looked up at me with the exact same ones so that suddenly it was like there was just no escape from ten green-blue circle-eyes seeing right through my claim to butchery and me seeing all that beauty in all of them. There was just no escape. I said to her, "You're right. You're exactly right. I'm not any kind of butcher at all. I'm just a man who sells meat."

"It must be very difficult for you," she said. "To be living that lie." And her voice was full of understanding, full of care. She ordered two pounds of ground round and I gave her ground sirloin instead, no extra charge.

My mother used to say only people who see you for what you are can truly love you. If they don't see you clearly, they're just looking in a mirror and loving themselves. I know she saw my father for what he was. "He was a butcher to his bones," she told me just before she died. "If he couldn't take it out on the cows, God alone knows what that man would have done to us. Oh, how I loved him . . ." Then she expired.

Delia Barrymore saw me for who I was. I didn't kid myself she loved me, but I loved her right away. She would come in on Tuesday afternoons between four thirty and five, and we would talk. She said she wanted to understand my relationship with meat. That she could tell it was complex. I told her about my father, and his father and his all the way back to Lil. She asked me to bring in the picture and I dug it out to show her. I described how I ran screaming from the family slaughterhouse as a child and never set foot in it again. How I knew I had let my father down, knew I didn't deserve to be called a butcher. That I was more like a mortician making the dead in my care look more palatable to viewers. That I felt like a fraud every day. We talked about what it would take to get Karl to take down the big red BUTCHER sign and put one up that said MEAT SELLER or PURVEYOR OF MEATS—her idea—or even just MEAT. "It doesn't have to be about me," I said. "Did you ever notice, it's the only sign in the market that's about the person working there? It should be about the meat." She told me she agreed. She said she had always loved meat, any meat. That she craved it constantly. She talked about how sometimes she was hungry for meat in the middle of the night. In the morning when she woke up. She used the word insatiable and then the word comestible and every moment we talked was a torture of desire—as though I was alive for the first time, as though I had been just another piece of dead flesh until she arrived to see into my heart, into my soul. As though I had never seen the value of inhabiting a living body until then. Of being a red-blooded American male. As she spoke, I imagined each part of her, like the drawing hanging on the wall, a dotted line between her hip and flank, her leg and butt, each section something to savor, to taste. She would come in, week after week, fewer and fewer children hanging off her all the while, until by the Tuesday after Presidents' Day, she was there all alone. It was her on one side of the counter, me on the other. Only meat between us. She picked out a rump roast and I wrapped my best tenderloin, keyed it in as soup bones. One dollar and seventy-nine cents. But before I could hand her the package, she said she'd mentioned something to Karl about the sign, that she'd told him she thought the word butcher was frightening for her children which was why she had stopped bringing them in, that she didn't believe it was a proper reflection of good family values to have a word on display that means killer, especially not on an enormous red sign—as though it were covered in the blood of the dead. And that she'd heard other mothers say the same. That local children were having difficulty with sleep, dreaming of a killer holding a huge sharp knife, lurking in Karl's Finer Food, often taking the form of Karl himself. Little sparks of spit flew from her mouth, bright and glittering, like there was some kind of flame inside of her. She said she'd told him it seemed highly preferable to them all, all the mothers, just to have a small sign, maybe blue with gold letters, that said MEAT. That the children's nightmares would surely stop. That the community would feel at peace. Then she stopped talking. She was barely looking at me then. Her cheeks were flushed. Her chest rose and fell with deep breaths. Ribs. Breasts. Shoulder. I gave her the tenderloin and I told her that I loved her. After all those months. I couldn't help myself. I told her it was really my heart that she held in her hands. And it was. She leaned toward me so her body pressed against the glass of the case. Two great big teardrops spilled from her eyes onto the white package in her hand; and for a moment we both stared at those salt water orbs, watching as they soaked into the paper brightness, dark circles appearing where each had sat, as though she had pressed her circle-eyes to the package of meat. And for just another moment I thought how lucky it was I hadn't used the heavy wax paper because then her tears might have rolled onto the floor and been stepped on by other customers instead of making something so beautiful, so perfect. "You should never have to lie about what you are," she said, and touched my hand. "I love you," she whispered. "But this is wrong." And then she left. Two days later, the BUTCHER sign was gone. By Friday, the new one was up, just like she'd described. Blue with gold lettering: MEAT.

＊　＊　＊

Delia Barrymore and I have never exchanged another word. She still comes to the counter on Tuesday afternoons, and I still give her the best meat I have, all the while charging her for tripe, but neither of us speaks. We don't have to. I know exactly what she wants. And she knows exactly who I am. She stands on one side of the meat case, me on the other, just like we've stood every time. Flesh between our flesh. Death surrounded by desire.

Insatiable. Comestible. Insatiable.

Found in the *Placebo*

The Yearbook of Emile Durkheim High School

CARL FRANKENSTEIN, CUSTODIAN

I am a big man, a big man with an unfortunate name. The embroidery on my uniform stretches way beyond the pocket, over-sews the placket. An ugly man who lives alone. A man who will not unlist his home phone number. A man who answers every phone call each night. "Frankenstein," I answer. I hear the murmuring laughs. At halftime of the basketball games, I lumber onto the hardwood with my wide furry mop, up and down the court. The students mob the stands, heave trash into my path. I circle, shaking my fists at the throng in the shadows of the bleachers, the monster that I am. Their monster. After the game, I walk home. I want to mop up the puddles of light cast by the streetlights, sop up the shadows the moon spills in the gutters. At home, I listen to WOWO radio. There are all the scores of all the basketball games in the state that night. I read the phone book by the fire, chanting those numbers. And before I go to bed, I rip out the stitches of my name from my uniform. Every last thread. I open that old incision over my heart.

CAROL APP, TRUANCY SECRETARY

All day, I make the calls. I check on absences. The rolls come in from the homerooms right after the first bell, collected by dedicated student aides, circulating through the contagious corridors and hallways. The stairwell sings and sewers. Names of the absent. The never-made-it-ins. I contact the contact numbers. I push the number buttons with the eraser on my pencil. No one is home. No one is ever home. Or, no, I imagine them at home in bed, the situation dire. So sick, so stricken that no one can reach the jangling phone on the table next to the sickbed. It rings and rings. Sometimes there are ghostly recordings, ghosts in the machine. "We can't make it to the phone right now . . ." I see them wasting away, sweaty in soiled sheets. The stench. The pestilence. Chronic illness is chronic. I put a check mark next to the names, a vector indicating that I will call them back. I call them back. I call them back. Receive the stutter of the persistent ring. Percussive pertussis. A buzz like a biting sting. Allergic to my ear. I am, sad to say, the only one who will receive, in the next hopeful spring, a certificate, one I will make myself, recognizing perfect perfect attendance.

LESLIE SANGUINE, CAFETERIA CASHIER

I believe everyone in the school, including the teachers, receives a free or reduced lunch. I am for show, running the old mechanical NCR register, registering the chits ringing up the dimes. Afterwards, I wipe the tables down, restore the order to the condiments, turning the catsup bottles into hourglasses, dripping what's left of one bottle into the leavings of the other. Gravity works, okay? I sweep up the litter of each day's notes that the kids' moms have packed with their cold lunches, little scraps of paper with messages, instructions, prayers. Half-baked home-baked sentiments, fortune cookie scribbles slipped in the pails and sacks. "Try to have a good enough day, Tim!" "Don't fret too much!" "Hope you do a better job in math." "Don't embarrass yourself or us!!!" Or sometimes just a penciled face. One big O with three little o's inside. Oh, oh, oh, oh. My other job—we all work other jobs—is restocking the greeting cards concessions in town. The rack at Blister's Pharmacy downtown. Rumi's Cigar Store. Rupp and Otting's Market, the Five and Dime, the newsstand in the courthouse run by the blind. I've noticed that the birthday cards, the ones for weddings, new births, anniversaries languish while the get-well ones and the cards of sympathy and bereavement fly out the doors. I work on commission. Pennies a card. After hours, on my hands and knees, I count out from the cartons the somber cards and their dour envelopes and count them into their predetermined slots on the racks. It is like another cafeteria line. Here you go. All the grief you can eat. One more fresh smorgasbord of sad sadnesses.

HOWARD JUNKER, FACILITIES ENGINEER

My friends call me "How." "How, how you do this?" I get asked all the time. I always know how. How to tape and mud the drywall. How to build a header and shim a doorframe. How to wire and plumb. How to snap a plumb line. How to fire the boilers, move the steam. How to make the clocks run on time. My workshop is a shack I built on the roof I roofed. There on my workbench all the guts of the appliances are spread out on the Masonite table I built from scratch. My tools, a silver Milky Way on pegboard. Coffee cans of fasteners. Tupperware tubs of fuses, switches, drawer pulls.

I know how to maintain. I know how to maintain. Look! Do you hear that? This mechanical calculator I salvaged from Mr. Rice's physics lab thirty years ago is still running. Big as a breadbox, studded and stuttering with gears and ratchets and armatures and levers, it has been sawing away all that time. Long ago, I told the machine to perform an impossible task. I divided a whole number by zero and the contraption's workings have been searching all this time (in the toothed flanges, greased widgets, stripped screws) for the mechanical expression of infinity. The machine makes a racket as it calibrates, clucking and clunking, at any moment on the edge of entropy, unengineering itself, a twitching pile of junk. But it goes on and on. How does it do it? I maintain it. I tend to it. It will keep looking for infinity forever. Forever forever. It is a little engine that asks how how how how. How's time machine telling time.

The Bottle

Something's curled up in the bottle. I don't want to look right at it.

Something makes the bottle knock.

It's Tuesday afternoon and the weather's asleep with its belly and long tail wrapped around the town. The curtains are hot with it.

I'm writing this yesterday.

I was going to write this from a distance, like I was God studying the classified ads of this town, old God scowling through his magnifying glass, God with long breaks for the bathroom, God sweating it out in polyester pants with the doors and windows locked against tweakers and Mexicans. God before he comes back in the second half as a long-haired teenager.

When we moved into this house the door was hanging from one hinge but the other side was heavy with bolts and chains just brushing the floor uselessly and the frame was busted. Someone had tried but couldn't lock someone out. We stayed at my grandma's till June, then moved after school ended. School's important to Ma. But that means we showed up here with nowhere to go, all day not knowing anybody. Ma works the half day at Target and half as a checker at Martin's and most nights she brings something home from the half-price barrel: hot dog buns, marshmallow fluff,

Miracle Whip a day or two off. And you have to wait a long time for Miracle Whip to go off.

I'm sure Noah took it with him in the ark, it's that practical. Maybe this very same jar.

And he didn't even have to wait in the ark that long. Not as long as summer vacation. And he had all the animals to talk to, though it must have smelled bad.

When school starts we'll get folders from Target, nice ones this year. Me and Tasmin already have ours picked out.

But then there's the bottle. It's thick like a jar with a big cork on the top. Moonshine maybe, Ma thought. We left it up there; it was too heavy to move. Just a couple of inches of liquid in the bottom that you couldn't tell what color it was supposed to be. The house also came with the pullout couch where Ma sleeps, the thin beds where Tasmin and me sleep, and a chest of drawers. So except for the door, it's nice here, and a man from church came and fixed the door and also hooked up the electric to a wire outside.

Tasmin disappears every morning before I can barely wake up. Tasmin's mean, which is lucky for her. Meanness is like a magic charm. It makes you hard, and hardness protects you. That's obvious. That's in any book (except the Bible). Tasmin is also half black, which is weird, because she's blonder than me, I mean her skin is blonde, and even her eyes are kind of blondey green. My hair and my skin are like soap or a dishcloth or anything plain you'd find around the house.

She's eleven and I'm thirteen.

I started it with the bottle. When I had looked at everything a million times, I sat on the couch and stared at the bottle up on its shelf until the air went thick between us. Then, inside the bottle, the liquid went a little thick and bulged. It sent up a bubble. I was so surprised I made a little noise out loud, it just bubbled out of me, and then the noise surprised me too. Suddenly the house felt so still and quiet I went out on the concrete and sat down. It was too hot for my bare legs. A bird was hopping around like the concrete was too hot for its feet. It kept turning its ear to the ground. It's supposed to hear worms that way. Living under the concrete, under the ground.

The next day after Ma and Tasmin cleared out I returned to the exact same spot on the couch and studied the bottle. It seemed a little fuller now. Sunlight was hitting it from somewhere high up, and the light hit little gold flecks and grains suspended in the liquid, which was now a definite green. The specks swirled around like dust swirled in the air. They swirled around and then spread out and then clenched back in again. Like something that lives deep in the water and not in a bottle on a shelf. It repeated this motion and repeated it. It was getting organized.

Then there was a knock at the door. It was the guy from church who fixed the door up in the first place. Steve he reminds me. How're you doing sweetheart? He says Hoo it's pretty hot in there you should keep this open.

He comes in and sits on the couch. I also sit on the couch and keep my side to the bottle so I don't have to watch it, but of course that side of my face feels fat and hot. He's talking about this and that, I don't know what, his own daughters, they live with their mama too up in White Pigeon. He bought this for one of them but it was too small, they've grown up so fast, what do you think, sugar? he says and he pulls out of this paper bag (I didn't notice before) a hot pink T-shirt. That gets my attention. It's printed with a shower of stars down the front, and the bottom is all fringed and fixed with beads, and instead of sleeves it has a knot on each shoulder and a couple of beads dangling from there too. He lays it flat on my lap. I pull at the beads. He asks why I don't try it on. Then something jumps up in my throat from my stomach, I don't know what, but it feels round and golden, and I can barely make a breath around it, but finally I gasp out Tomorrow, I'll try tomorrow and he pats my knee. He says, all right then, sweetheart, I'll be by tomorrow, and I'll bring some Cokes. But put that special shirt away, don't let your sister or your mama know about it, that's just for you. And that's it he's gone out the door.

My heart is beating like a rotten pond, like what's in the bottle, and my ankles are shaky when I get to my feet. I don't look at the bottle, but now's when I hear it knock. Or is that just my heart, trying to shake me, trying to beat me up from the inside? Why is my heart mad at me? Why is the bottle? I don't want to look. I feel like just looking would hit me in the face.

But I run to our bedroom and I try on the shirt. It's all spangled and reflects light. It hangs down my chest like a shield with hearts. I wear it for a while, and then I stuff it way down between the sheets in my bed. Then I lie on my bed for the rest of the day, until I hear Tasmin bang in.

And then the next morning I put on my shirt and sit on my bed as the silence in the house goes all thick. I pull my hair back on top which makes me look older. Sunlight cuts in the dirty windows and the curtains too. Dust swirls around the light like it can't get satisfied. I wish I had my ears pierced and some earrings.

I'm listening but I don't hear the knocking of the bottle just something that taps in my own head quiet and steady like Tasmin messing with me trying to make me mad. I feel a little mad. My madness is small like a little fire made of the points of needles, a gold fire like I've never seen. I pick it up and it tinkles like a chain.

I tie the fire around my throat and it goes inside and makes a weird fat ring under the skin. It holds my neck up and my chin up pointy and stiff like a princess's. I stand and walk all slowly into the next room. My T-shirt is gone and my gown is hanging down all around me yellow and heavy and my neck is bulging. The next room is full of a yellow light. It's coming from the middle of the room. There's a huge yellow glow there, and floating in the middle of the glow is a yellow lizard and a yellow baby. They're the same person. His tail bends forward under a pair of stunted little baby legs with claws that crab the air. There's a rash of pale yellow bumps up the back of his tail. His big baby belly's like a frog's belly I can see a vein in and two little arms just lie on the belly, and then there's his huge head like something came out of the oven wrong, the part that holds the brains is all piled up on the forehead in big folds, and his head's so heavy his neck bends forward in a curve, and there's a slick of yellow pond slime over the eyes. He sneezes and I can see he has these wounds on both sides of its head like three slashes healing over. Who cut this big messy baby? It's not a cute baby but it's helpless like a rotten onion.

Then there's a knocking, knocking, knocking at the door and I run for the baby. When I reach him I'm instantly dirty from my hair to my feet in a cold and sticky muck. All I can see is glow so I wave my arms around crazy and feel for the baby. The baby's laughing in my ears like nickels but I also hear the knocking knocking and I know it's Steve. Coming, coming! I say but already my feet can't move and I'm feeling around my knees for the baby, is he hiding there? Coming, coming! I say but I can't bend down any more, just stick my arms straight out and move them in circles, hoping to catch at the baby. Coming, coming I try to say but the glow stuffs my mouth and it rings like nickels. Then I feel something press at both my ears and wrench my neck and face toward the door. Pond scum stretches from my eyes to the door, and then it burns through the door to where Steve is standing with a nice smile on his face. Then my eyes burn out his smile and his face falls away and I can see his skull and his teeth smiling like on a poison bottle and I know that's a message for me. Then his collar's on fire and a little bit of the tree branch that was hanging over his head and then the skull starts shaking in midair and I can see his spine like a stem flexing in the fire of his shirt and it sways and it sways and then it collapses in a pile and the fire snuffs out instantly though this sour smoke is rising neatly and symmetrically from the little pile in all directions.

Then all of a sudden I can move again and my old mad feeling comes back and it's shaking inside of me like a million gold chains and all the words come into my head that Tasmin calls me when Ma's not around. I fly to where the door used to be. I look down on this pile of ash and dirt and I just start pounding it with my feet. Steve you motherfucker, Steve! What did you do to the door, Steve? Steve you slut asshole. What did you do to the *door*?

Then I go in and fill up the spaghetti pot with water and come back and dump it on the step and the little pile is gone though the step is streaky black. Then I keep doing it until this streaky black is gone.

Then I go back and sit on the couch. The door is gone except for the knob and hinges which sit on the ground, but I don't look at them. I'm looking at the shelf, where the bottle used to be. Now with nothing on it. My sexy T-shirt is gone too, burned off me, and I can feel a breeze on my bare skin, and a breeze inside, too, a kind of rising. Where the baby's gone, where the baby's going to be.

Deanne Stovers

Wayne is a good man. I'm lucky to get him. People keep telling me those things, as if I need reminding. He took care of his troubled sister from the time he was nineteen years old, tracking her more than once to the houses where she was shooting up and taking her back home. Wayne's youth was sacrificed on the altar of that girl. I should be grateful that a man like that wants to marry me now, when the skin under my eyes is showing lines and the legs that used to look slim and good in shorts now just look like stalks. I am grateful. But shouldn't a man have wanted a little more out of his life? Shouldn't a man have taken some time off from his mess of a sister once in a while, going out to the quarry with a few guns and friends who've been drinking? He took care of her to the day she died, and after. He was the one to wash her body for the funeral. People talked.

This is exactly why I need to wear a white dress, even if white makes me look little and washed out. Mama said I could pass for a used cotton ball. She thinks I should have a pink wedding gown. She thinks I look good in pink, which is true, but she forgets that white means something. I'm not talking about how I've had other boyfriends. Everybody in town knows that. White means respect for the tradition, and I'm trying to get this right.

I have thoughts that are not helpful. What does it mean that a man who spent ten years chasing down his sister in shooting galleries thinks that marrying me is the natural next move? Mama tells me not to say such things. I don't see why I shouldn't. Everybody who saw me pulling in to park at Monica's Bridal did.

I tried on a dress that Wayne would like—strapless, with lots of flounces on the skirt. The salesgirl had to pin it to hold it up, chattering, "Aren't you tiny! Not many of the girls who come in are so little." I looked in the mirror and saw a broomstick rising from a mound of whipped cream. "Maybe something with sleeves," I said to her, while Mama said, "You can always dye it pink." She was trying to make this a happy day. One look at her face told me she was remembering my first day of school, my first bike—the days before every room started to seem too small. Once she sent me to school in a turtleneck, and by the time I got home I'd cut out the neck with craft scissors.

I'm too old now to wear a dress designed for a twenty-year-old and Wayne must know that. He's not a fool and he doesn't close his eyes when he looks at me. He says, "I like a girl who's been around the block." Well, he shouldn't. He should stand up straighter and get mad enough to snarl at the girl he's going to marry when she comes home later than she said she would, and drunk besides. When she lets the guys she works with tease her that the fella she's marrying is fussy as an old lady. Wayne shrugs and says, "People say things," and then he asks me what I want for dinner. Sometimes the words are right there in my mouth: "Oh, grow a pair." He fusses at me, tucking in my scarf and putting Chapstick on my lips so I don't have to dig through my purse for gloss. His eyes are calm when he does these things. He loves to tuck in my scarf.

I was barely fourteen when I went joyriding with Neil Osterman. He was nineteen, and I knew where we were going and what we were going to do there, and I yelled, "Faster!" whenever he slowed down. By the time we got to the quarry he was leaving rubber at every corner, including the one where we'd spun out and got a grill full of green corn. Drunk, of course, both of us, and loud, hollering as we swung on the rope over the glassy water. People think that Neil's drunk hands slipped on the rope and he fell onto the boy swimming below us, but it wasn't so simple. Neil was bombing for him and I was hanging onto Neil, screaming either "Go! Go!" or "No! No!" The versions vary. I'd been drinking too. Was that my sin, or was it the two of us, slick and wet teenage bodies, landing on that little boy, or was it me holding my head up after the funeral that every soul in Winesburg seemed to turn out for? My other sin was continuing to ride with Neil until he got locked up.

Wayne knows all of this. I made sure. I don't want him coming home from the NAPA shop one day with his mouth folded back against the words he doesn't want to say to me. He wants to protect me, even now.

"Do you still love Neil? Is that it?" Mama had demanded after she heard that I turned down Wayne a second time. Of course I don't love Neil. It was Neil's house that Wayne hauled his sister out of. Without even trying I can conjure Neil's lazy sneer. He liked to blow cigarette smoke in my mouth when we kissed. No woman in her right mind loves Neil.

The salesgirl brought me another dress, with lacy sleeves that ate at my arms like a tracing of fire ants. The lace rode up in a high collar. "You won't be able to fasten this yourself, but your mama can help you," the salesgirl said. Mama looked unhappy. What did she think we were buying, a party dress? The lace pinched, so stiff I could barely bend my elbows.

"Look at you! A bride!" the salesgirl said.

In the mirror stood a girl, skinny as a needle, her skin gray underneath the stupid white lace.

"You'll be wrapped up too tight to dance at your own wedding," Mama said.

The salesgirl started to talk about alterations and Mama was saying pink, both of them chattering until I said, "Hush," as if I had a right.

"Are you crying?" Mama said.

"That's tears of joy," the salesgirl said. "I see them a lot."

"You keep thinking that," I said. My arms were too stiff at my sides to wipe my eyes, so a drop landed on the dress, spotting it and making it mine now.

Gregg Pitman

The third "g," the double on the end, is not a misspelling. That is how you spell my name. I am a bastard. My father was a visiting stenography instructor, my night school mother's teacher at Winesburg's Business Athenaeum. I was conceived in the simulated office suite on the second floor whose desks had all been graffitied with the swooping swooshes and schwa strokes of its students studying shorthand. In short, shorthand became my first language. With the sharpened red-painted nail of her index finger, my mother, never speaking, transcribed what she was thinking on my belly or on my back as I learned to toddle or on my butt as she changed me. In shorthand, she annotated me with her abbreviated and compressed baby talk in the style of the gestural dingbats, curlicues, and ellipses of this our secret shared language. My growth was stunted by this stunted dialect, abbreviated, and, at the same time, accelerated as shorthand was built for speed. I never, really, learned to speak—my grammar truncated, my vocabulary condensed, the syntax reduced like a roux—but I did learn to listen. Listen: I turned out to have the gift of anticipation. I am a kind of hobbled psychic who only foresees a few seconds into the future, enough to change the story before it is told or, at least, to get the gist of the gist down on paper. It was only natural that I ended up doing what I am doing now. I'm the municipality's court reporter, a freelance clerk at all the depositions, a civil servant, an auxiliary in the interrogation rooms of the constabulary, recording the endless confessions of the long-winded citizenry whose secrets of incest, abuse, murder, rape, and torture pile up in the coded squiggles and squirms of my spiral-bound oblong pads. At night in my shotgun shack on the West End, I reread the traumatic digestions of trauma, note how all these horrific acts have been transformed, strike that, I meant to say tamed, by their abstraction into the innocent scratches of a child pretending to write. I cannot sleep. Or when I do, I dream of a writhing orgiastic montage of writing run amuck. I wake to moonlight. There, crescent moon is a silent letter in the shorthand of the universe. It stands for "and" or "but" or "or." Sleepless, I compose grosses of bad news letters for the front office of the Winesburg Knitting Mill, using the supplied templates of boilerplate text, leaving blank the spaces for the recipient and the sender to be supplied by the cursive endless longhand of the anonymous signatory.

Mari, Waiting

A wife waits for her husband, a wife waits for her husband.

Mari whose name is not Mari waits for Gus whose name is not Gus.

(Mary waits for Gursnan.)

Mari waits for Gus, her husband, though she's not yet used to the word.

A *wife* waits at the window for her *husband,* though they have not uttered these terms since the interview.

A wife in contract but not in covenant, a wife in status, a wife in stasis, a wife in ink and pixel—not loin, not bone—a wife like scissors for red tape, a wife beneath a loophole arbor dripping with marsh marigolds and lady's slipper and pasture roses worn wide by a pageant of loveless lovers walking arm in arm, waits.

Mari waits for Gus at the window, practicing—*This is Gus, my* husband. *My* husband *has not eaten for twenty days. My* husband *does not plan to eat for fifteen more.*

A wife waits for her husband to come home from a run.

Mari waits at the sink while Gus—twiggy brown hull—jogs in slow motion, jogs as an old man windup toy might jog, jogs as Go-Go Gandhi might if Gandhi had a new pair of Brooks

Adrenaline GTS 12s, jogs into Winesburg and out the other side, though his *wife* has asked him not to jog there.

Mari waits and waiting with her is Gus, the ghost of him, the cartoon silhouette: short, silky and regal purple running shorts, and beneath those his special cotton underwear which pokes out the bottom a little and has a drawstring, his bare boy's chest, his tiny lavender nipples, his pinched taut abdomen, his hard outie, his black mist of beard, his lovely and bulbous marigold turban with its secret wooden comb tucked inside, his brown legs pistons, his brown arms thew, his go belt strapped around his hips, hung with plastic globules filled with water and his crescent dagger in its sheath, his polished silver kara around his wrist, tinking lightly against his stopwatch.

Though she has asked him not to, Gus jogs frail past the county park and the Catholic school and the Winesburg Diner and the Dollar General and the closed Circuit City where they were best friends before they were play pretend spouses and Karl's Finer Food and Martin's Grocery and the house where Mari grew up with her mother inside making ham salad and sighing over the curious decisions of an undutiful daughter and the slaughterhouse and the Target glowing in the dusk like all those spaceships landed in all those cornfields, while Mari waits.

Mari waits at the end of the driveway with a fresh, sweating water bottle, a few drops of lemon juice added in secret.

In secret, Mari waits for Gus, waits to pluck the cicadas from his sweat-glistening back, waits to scoop the gnats from his eyes.

Mari waits and waits and waits while duallies downshift and open up the sky and thunder too near Gus, waits while boys she went to high school with shout *Raghead,* and *Faggot,* and *Sand nigger.*

Mari—kneeling at the tub, rinsing in hot water yards and yards of supple saffron fabric which sway like water plants, losing and finding her hands in them, scraping with her square, unpainted fingernails crusted pink flagella where a gallon of strawberry ice cream launched from a Cummins diesel detonated in front of Gus, recalling how he came home early with fat carpenter bees wafting behind him, recalling how she had wanted very badly to lick him clean—waits.

Mari at the window, Mari at the drive, Mari at the bathtub and Mari in the bedroom, stringing damp fabric to dry around the room where the night before Gus stood in his special cotton underwear—a gift from God. But wasn't everything?—telling how the knot at the drawstring was there to thwart lustful thoughts, to remind the faithful to think of members of the opposite sex as they would a family member, *Like you, Mari, you're like a sister to me,* then Gus unknotting the knot and saying how to test himself, Gandhi used to sleep nude with his grandniece, and holding Mari from behind, Gus sliding his smooth penis up and down between her fat-dappled butt cheeks, waiting.

Mari waits for Gus to leave her, Mari waits for Gus to love her.

Mari waits for Gus to stand up too quickly, waits for him to faint, because when he falls he falls silent as a pile of laundry and she sits on the floor and puts his swaddled head in her lap and kisses him.

Mari waits, though for what she does not know.

"Manchild" Morrison
The Best That Almost Was

Every ten years they trot me out for homecoming. Put me in the back of a red convertible and drive me around the stadium where half a century ago I took the Railsplitters to our first and only state championship. We ran the single wing back then, the old "Pop" Warner formation, with four guys in the backfield, any one of us ready for the snap. But in 1962, in Winesburg, Indiana, everyone knew the ball was going to number 21. I might as well have had a target on my jersey.

I don't remember how I got the nickname "Manchild." It used to drive my mother crazy.

He's Donald, for the love of Pete.

What are you feeding him, Mrs. Morrison?

Her Irish cheeks would glow as red as twisted apples.

I was always big for my age. A twelve-pound baby, a head taller than my classmates in all the pictures. In seventh grade I played varsity basketball. In eighth the football coach suited me up, and the rest is history. To this day I hold every school record: rushing touchdowns, touchdown passes, all-purpose yards. I have all the kicking records, too. Once, before practice, I knocked a fifty-eight yarder through the goalposts, but it wasn't such a feat: the wind was at my back and the ball nicked the crossbar on its way through.

He's just being modest, people would say when I'd tell them I wasn't that good, but it turned out I was right. Never made the pros. Ask anyone outside the county if they've heard of "Manchild" Morrison and you'll get a nod from a Purdue diehard or two who remembered the hype that followed my signing. "The Best That Almost Was," ran the headline in the *Indianapolis Star* the week after I blew out my knee in a scrimmage freshman year.

People tell me I would have played alongside Bob Griese, another in-state hotshot who would go on to All American, then quarterback for the Miami Dolphins, winner of two Super Bowls and owner to this day of the last undefeated season in pro football.

Undefeated. Imagine.

I never did finish at Purdue. Got the surgery, but doctors were stabbing in the dark in 1963. They stapled the ends of the ligament together and one afternoon, on a rehab jog around the track, I felt a ping, then collapsed on the asphalt. I was no Gale Sayers. I wasn't coming even halfway back from that. So I dropped out and headed home to Winesburg, sat around for a year or two feeling sorry for myself, gained forty pounds on sympathy casseroles. I hung a map of the U.S. on my bedroom wall, put pins in the states I'd visited— the Great Lakes eight, plus four in the south from a family trip to New Orleans. Twelve down, thirty-eight to go. Then the center on the old team, Tommy Flynn, who had just finished up at DePauw, proposed we go into business together. All I had to do was lend my name and look the part of local legend, and we'd have it made.

"Manchild" Motors: New and Used. Tommy was right, for a time. We did a good business. I worked the door, he did the selling, and his sunny wife, Cheryl, kept the books. They had twin boys and bought a five-bedroom house on a man-made lake in

Whispering Woods. But one day, out for a test drive (he loved to see which was the fastest car on the lot), Tommy flipped a Camaro on the river road and went off to join James Dean. I was left with a car dealership, a grieving widow, and little idea of what to do with either. Six months after the funeral, Cheryl and I were going over inventory in her office when she put her hand on my cheek. I still remember the photo on her desk of Tommy and the kids peering at us, as if through a window. We married, divorced, remarried, and now we're separated again. I haven't spoken with her since spring.

Which brings me more or less to this morning, when I found myself standing at the bathroom mirror of the Extended Stay in my fifty-year-old high school uniform, the 21 as yellow as my teeth against the faded crimson. Coach Keller Jr. had asked me to the wear the old jersey again. He'd done the same for the fortieth-anniversary homecoming, as had his dad, Coach Keller Sr., for the thirtieth, twentieth, and tenth. I'll admit that I've tried on the uniform over the years, and not just before these games. But it never fit, so in the past I went in a windbreaker with the dealership's logo on the back—a red Mustang flying through goalposts.

This time, though, the jersey slid right on. In fact, it drooped over my shoulders and arms; I looked like an old man playing dress-up. If I'd opened the door to such a sight on Halloween, I'd have felt a shiver. The whole town would be there. Cheryl. The twins, their wives and kids. No one missed a homecoming, and this was the golden anniversary of the once and forever golden age. I've seen more people in the dealership over the last few months than I have in years. But they haven't been buying cars. They go online or drive to volume lots in Indy or Fort Wayne. I used to move fifty cars a month. Now I'd be lucky to sell five. I should have changed the name years ago. People who actually watched

"Manchild" Morrison smash through a defensive line and drag cornerbacks downfield like strings of cans are dying every week. Parents. Uncles and aunts. Teachers. Shopkeepers. Classmates. I used to go to their memorials but lately I'd rather not be seen.

It was Cheryl who first mentioned the weight loss. She made me stand on her bathroom scale. Two hundred forty, down twenty pounds from normal. I hadn't been to the doctor in five years, and my refusal after the scale's needle kept marching west—now under two hundred for the first time since I was a kid—opened up old hurts in Cheryl that made her impossible to live with. Anything would set her off. A coffee mug I hadn't rinsed out. Empty trash cans too long at the curb. The way I'd forget to switch stations when commercials came on. *Earth to Donald,* she said. And when I still wouldn't go to the doctor after months of Cheryl's nagging, she gave me one last chance. Called in the appointment herself, wrote it down in big letters on the kitchen calendar. *11:30 AM. Dr. Reeves. You go, or I go,* she said. *I'm not going to be a widow two times over.*

I went to work, and I swear I had every intention of driving over to the internist's. But I had a customer who was hot to buy a new Chrysler 300, and we were negotiating, me holding firm, stepping away to the back office to stall the guy. It was noon when we closed the deal, my first and last of that week. Cheryl asked me to move out the next day.

I haven't stepped on a scale since, but I can feel myself shrinking. I drove forty-five miles to the outlet mall to buy clothes that would fit, and the expressions of people who come into the dealership tell me all I need to know. They're too polite to ask, *What happened to the rest of you?* Or to say, *You're getting treatment, I assume?* I don't trust doctors, but that's not the real issue. If I made another appointment, if I stood up in the waiting room when the nurse called, *Mr. Morrison,* and went through that door to the steel table, I'd be interrupting the natural course of events. I remember Cheryl once asking, *Do you ever wonder what would have happened if you hadn't played in that scrimmage, or if the ball had gone to someone else on that particular down? You might not have come home. We might never have met. Tommy and I might have been watching you on TV, inviting people over on Sundays to brag on you and talk about the '62 team.*

I don't think about that stuff, I said. *What's meant to be is meant to be.*

I remember another time, after I'd dropped out of college, my mother coming into my room one afternoon when I'd been sleeping most of the day.

What are you going to do? she asked.

I guess we'll see what happens, I said.

You sound just like your father.

How would I know?

My father drove a '51 Windsor convertible. My mother used to call it his mistress. The lady in red. I was too young to understand what she meant, but I can picture him now, out on the driveway polishing the hood, bent close enough to see his reflection. Just as my mother might have predicted, he did run off with that car. He used to talk about California, but he only got as far as Casper, Wyoming, before he ran out of money or nerve. He did roustabout work in the oil fields, made journeyman then foreman at the Amoco refinery, died of a heart attack on the job nine months short of retirement.

I don't know if Coach Keller has heard the details of that story—surely so, in a town like this—but of all the cars on the lot he always asks me to bring a red convertible for my little halftime parade around the track. And I say sure. But this year I must have forgotten to order a red convertible because the only soft top we have in stock is black, with tinted windows. I grab the keys, toss the old jersey in the passenger seat, and fire up the engine. Though it's a perfect fall evening, I keep the top up for now. It's eight o'clock. Homecoming Friday. The streets are dim and empty. Closed signs glow in the restaurant windows. I could run the red lights, strip naked and race down Main Street crying *Hallelujah,* and no one would see or care because they're all at the football stadium.

By the time I drive up near the entrance, it's late in the second quarter and the place is packed to the gills. I cut the motor, crack the window to let in the cool breeze, the smell of popcorn, cotton candy, raked leaves, and hormones. The crack of helmets and pads, waves of cheers, whistles, air horn blasts sweep in. The school band, forever out of tune, plays "We Will Rock You" and cheerleaders shoot into the air like fireworks. Coach Keller paces the sidelines, tugging at his headset. And I can see gathered behind him, lined up in the stands, some of the old-timers—my teammates—wearing their faded jerseys. A few of them are shifting around, seeming anxious, as if on the lookout for someone.

The universal rule of homecoming games is that you schedule a team you can beat, but the Railsplitters are down 24–3. I'm checking the clock on the scoreboard and getting ready to pop the top of the convertible—I've already got my fingers on the release handle—when I see one of the old-timers point in my direction. He must have ESP because I'm a good fifty yards away in a hearse-black car with tinted windows double-parked outside the chain-link fence. Then someone else is looking over and others are pointing, too, and it's like I'm watching a Western in slow motion about a posse of retired lawmen who have come together for one last ride. They've stepped off the bleachers and are walking toward me, coming around the track, past the end zone and the concession stand. I let go of the release handle and turn the ignition. Before I roll up the window, I reach into the passenger seat and grab my old jersey. I toss the thing out onto the sidewalk, where it lands flat on its back, arms stretched out, as if steamrolled by tacklers.

I throw the car in drive and floor it. I peel out of there like a joyriding teenager. Squealing tires. Fishtailing. Leaving marks on the street. I don't slow down for lights or anything. I fly through town out to the river road, and up the ramp to the interstate, headlights stiff-arming the darkness. Nothing in front of me but open lanes, an empty map. I step on the gas, like Tommy Flynn, like the "Manchild" Morrison of old: football star. Can't stop me now. I'm going, going. Good as gone.

Carol Clay

I look out for strays, and when I find them I take them in. Our town of Winesburg has rows of telephone poles, rows of electricity poles. The wires go every which way. All wood, these poles, and I find my darlings clinging there, their little claws dug deep in the pine, girdled around at the same height like scallops of bark on a tree. There is nothing sadder than the messages. Have you seen the ones that say: Have you seen our Socks? Our Tom? Our Kitty?? That ask: Have you seen Mr. Mittens?? Or the ones that simply spell out LOST! or Reward!? Then they go on to say (I need my glasses for this) what color and how old and what special markings and last seen and call us anytime and we are sad and we miss miss miss miss. I can't have enough of the missing. I pry them free. I have a little flathead screwdriver to work under the staple. I don't tear the paper. I'm allergic to the real thing, to the real cat. But I fill my little house with these cats with their ghost-gray coats coating the pictures of the fliers. I have X-actoed them from the sad news of their departure. Look at that one yawning. That one's eyes are flashed with light. That one covered with yarn. Asleep in the sun. Batting a potted plant. Whaling on a keyboard. All wet from a bath. I have albums of the missing. In stacks and stacks throughout my bungalow, the books themselves like cats warming themselves near the registers, curled up on the couch, scratching at the door. I have papered the walls with the paper—a choir, shingles singing, mewing, purring. I open the door and the wall ruffles, rustles, twitches, arches its back in the draft. Its fur stands up. The fur flies. In some places, the paper is several layers deep, and I can flip through and make the kitties move, the still pictures fitting together into a movie in my brain. They lick themselves and stretch. They chase a bug. They roll and scratch. I go to the library to make more copies of my copies. I look sad. I've lost my cat. I am an old woman who has lost her cat. See, I show them. Have you seen Puddin'? They help me make copies of my copies. I put the pile in my red wagon. It is like walking a big red cat on a leash. Along the way, I look at all the poles, looking for new posters that ask me to look for missing cats. A tabby. A calico. Black cat. White cat. Long hair. Short. A Siamese. A Maine Coon. I have my little screwdriver to pry out the staple, to jimmy out the thumbtacks. I can't get enough. I paper over the windows of my bungalow with pictures of cats looking out the window. What are they looking at? Those cats are the inside cats. And I have taped more cats, outside cats, on the windows outside looking in at the inside cats. Cats are so curious. There are scare cats in my garden to scare the real cats away. Some pictures I have have more than one cat in them. Only one cat is missing but there are other cats pictured who aren't missing. I have found them all. The mommy cat who's nursing a brood of baby cats that now are all my cats. There are cats playing together. There are cats looking at goldfish in the goldfish bowl. Cats pawing at the refrigerator, at a bird flying by, at a child staring in. Many cats are sleeping. The big furry heads drooping. Ears are twitching in dreams. Tails flicking at the tip. Look, there the claws are extended. The cat is kneading. The outside light shines through the paper on the windows and pictures of cats curled up in a beam of sunlight curl up in the beam of sunlight cast through the window shadowed with pictures of cats chasing shadows. I have found all of these lost cats. The ones weathering on the light poles, on the telephone poles. I take pictures of the pictures and put the pictures in my albums, tape the pictures on the wall. When I am at the library, I copy the copy of a copy's copy. Each time the image of the cat licking its paw fades. It fades and fades. The light in the machine licks back and forth. The copy's copy grays, breaks up into finer and finer pieces, shades and shades and shades and shades of gray. At night, I sleep in a bed made up with a bedding of lost cats, paper I have pieced together, page by page, into a quilted comforter of sleeping napping cats, a thrumming blanket. In the dark, I feel them nestle in next to me, hear them crinkle and crimp as I move as they move to nuzzle my ear, bat my hair. They fill in the hollows all around me. They flatten and slide beneath me. They surround me like a skin. They are my fur. They ride on my chest, lighter than light. They rise and fall as I breathe, finding in all the layers and layers of loss a way to be found.

Triple Crown

She says it's like pulling teeth to get your kids to talk with you. Well, I've never believed that, not even before I got the new job. Maybe I'm lucky, but Jerrod and Jenny have always talked. Sometimes too much, yet I can't complain since they inherited blabbing from their mother. Life is good at home, not ideal, but pretty good. We converse over dinner every night. We watch a little TV after their homework. On weekends we take little trips.

Now the neighbor's kids, they're another story. Little sneaks. Hardened criminals waiting to happen, if you ask me. Really, what can you expect with a mother who covers up for them, who doesn't have the slightest respect for personal property? This isn't my kind of community, I'll tell you straight off—only a temporary landing pad between divorce and moving into a decent place with Ronny. A neighborhood of tacky rental houses—I knew it wasn't a good sign, but I have to pay off student loans, so I keep reminding the kids this is an "interim solution." A person can tolerate almost anything for a short time. Almost anything.

When we find the smashed-to-smithereens window in Ronny's truck, we know it has to be that older brat next door. Sheila showed my Jenny and Jerrod the slingshot her uncle gave her. "Uncle," that kind of sly nicknaming can confuse kids, since he sleeps in the same bed as their mom. Do they think Sheila's never heard of sex? Why don't they say "boyfriend"? Ronny and me, we're right out in the open, explaining to the kids that once legal matters get sorted, we'll make them ring bearers at the wedding. Well, you see what I mean about blabbing.

It wouldn't be so bad if it wasn't his *new* truck—something Ronny's been eyeing for a year, just stenciled with the logo of his construction company emerald green on both doors of the cab. He was so proud of Eleanora—he likes to name things, an odd habit, but harmless. His favorite hammer is Arnold. Ronny has a cute sense of humor to go with his cute body and complement his dark good looks. My kids love him. Even my *mother* loves him. Anyway, the window was one of those tinted black wing things that's going to cost half a month's rent in this dumpy house.

"Let it go," Ronny says. "It's not worth hassling over."

But the adrenaline is pumping kathump, kathump, and I march right over there and ask if she's going to take responsibility for her daughter's carelessness. (I never think the kid did it on purpose. She doesn't seem coordinated enough to hit a target.) I ask straight out, "Are you going to replace the window?"

So guess what she says.

"How do we know it was Sheila's fault?" The smile is a little sly, but her teeth are perfect, even, white teeth, the nicest thing about her.

"Well, how about: she's the only one around here toting a slingshot."

"Who says the window was broken by a slingshot? And if it was, who's to say other kids don't have this ordinary toy?"

Ordinary toy? How about "lethal weapon"? Of course I don't waste time arguing with Mrs. Perry Mason. We can't get a forensic report for a rock. So I say to her, "Let me give you some advice. You take that slingshot back and watch your Sheila and Brian because Ronny is a big man with a temper and you don't want *him* coming here next time."

Which is an outrageous lie because Ronny is a puppy; what would you suppose of a man who calls his hammer Arnold? But she doesn't know this.

I should have expected her reply.

"Kids these days, it's like pulling teeth to get them to talk with you."

In one sentence she insults my intelligence and my profession. If I were a nicer person, I'd try to get to know the woman. She's obviously down on her luck. But I'm overwhelmed trying to understand people and this particular neighbor has been such a pain. It's time to leave.

I've always been lucky with Jenny and Jerrod, always assured them they could tell me anything. And I've been honest—when I was fed up with cutting hair and wanted a more challenging job, I *told* them the dental tech training would squeeze our family budget. You know what Jenny said? She declared, "You have to follow your dreams, Mom." Imagine. She was eight at the time; that was four rocky, exciting, hectic years ago.

I am a lot happier now. And a better mother for it. My favorite part is making these temporary crowns. You have to get the mold just right, trust me. You mix so much liquid with the composite, fill the shell, pat it down evenly. Let it solidify. Then gently, very gently, release it. Combination chef and sculptor, that's how I see the work. Art, in its own small way. Of course some days here, the job is just cavity after cavity, filling after filling, where Dr. Carl does all the creative stuff and I spray and suck with tubes. Those days I feel more like a plumber.

Hey, I got sidetracked: the good news is that Ronny's insurance paid for most of the window, and the delinquents, Sheila and Brian, have been lying low for a while.

Naturally, family life isn't quiet for long. No, nothing to do with my drunken ex. He was relieved to be erased from the family photo—will probably erase himself altogether with the vodka. And although he never paid a cent of child support, he doesn't bother the kids or me. Truthfully, I do wonder how they feel about losing their dad, but Ronny is a much better father than Norman ever was—taking them to movies, for country rides in Eleanora. They love sitting high in the cab. And I *do* worry about leaving them alone on school holidays when I have to work. Even though they're super responsible and I was out babysitting at Jenny's age.

Listen to this story. I'm here last Wednesday. Seven to four as usual, and it's some kind of teacher's holiday or convention, so the kids are off school. I've planned ahead. Ronny says he'll swing by for lunch, teasing that Jenny's a better cook than I am. I've rented two videos for the kids, which they've promised not to watch until they finish their homework. Cross-your-heart isn't necessary because Jenny is president of the Math Club (doesn't get it from me; can't imagine she gets it from Norman) and Jerrod is the best writer in his class. I'm not saying my kids are junior Albert Einsteins, but they *like* school, you know. Well, I call them at 11 AM, between a simple filling and an impacted wisdom tooth (not my favorite assignment). Sure enough, all's quiet on the home front. Doing fine, Mom. Don't worry. Yes, we'll call if there's a problem.

It's a big day at the office. At 1 PM, a woman comes in for a triple crown, the three front teeth on the top row. She's a young person, too, twenty-eight, maybe twenty-nine. You never know about teeth and age. Some eighty-year-olds could do Colgate commercials. And some gals like this twentysomething—because of childhood poverty or stupid parents or bad calcium genes—just have rotten teeth. Obviously we don't use words like "rotten." We say "seriously compromised" or "diseased," or . . . In any event, I need to get this right, even if it is a temporary. You don't want her going out in the world looking like Bela Lugosi. Marie, that's her name, a smart girl, a nurse, tries not to be anxious. Dr. Carl removes the broken fillings, drills away crumbly bits of enamel. I'd never tell her how sad those teeth look waiting for the crowns. Little orphans, and of course they're super sensitive; we're so close to the nerves.

Marie's not afraid of the drill or hoses or even the pain, maybe because she's also a health professional. But I can tell she's nervous about her appearance. Well, *isn't everybody?* We had one fifty-year-old salesman make us refit a back bottom molar four times because he didn't like the porcelain match. Nobody's going to see that faraway tooth besides his lover or his doctor. But we cheerfully obliged.

I can hardly believe my ears when Dr. Carl declares, "Don't worry, Rhonda here is an artist when it comes to temporary crowns. You'll walk out today looking like a million dollars." He's not a man of words, Dr. Carl, and I have to tell you that praise makes me pretty happy. Still, I maintain a steady hand and concentrate slowly on the task. In the end, well, I don't think it's right to say we improve on Mother Nature, but Marie does have a lovely smile when she looks in the hand mirror.

Just as Marie's leaving, Marge comes up and says I should call home. My breath catches. Of course Marge was right not to interrupt during that delicate procedure, especially when Jenny tells her no, it's not an emergency.

I don't make a proper farewell to Marie, but we'll see her in two weeks when the permanent crown arrives. I'm rushing over to the phone. No emergency, I remind myself. Of course the line is busy the first time I dial. And the second. I stare at the picture of Lake Superior on Marge's wall calendar. Finally I get through. Jerrod answers. Doesn't have a clue why Jenny has phoned and takes an *age* to find her in that tiny house.

The kids have *never* called me at work before and my head is spinning. Maybe some Children's Welfare snoop has come by and found them home alone. I wouldn't put it past Sheila's mother, the stay-at-home-do-nothing busybody, to report me. Or maybe something's wrong with Ronny and he's told Jenny not to make a big deal of it when she calls. Construction is a dangerous job, especially when you're working alone. Those big beams. The sharp tools.

Jenny's sniffling and I have to ask her to speak up.

"You can tell me anything, honey."

"Yes, Mom, I know. Still, you're gonna be mad."

Oh, God, please don't let it be one of those meddling social workers.

"It's OK, honey, just tell me." I look at my watch because we have two more fillings before I can quit at 4 PM.

"Well, Sheila and I were playing tetherball in the backyard."

I might have known it. Sheila. Concentrating on the photo of Lake Superior, I imagine myself on a North Shore vacation, relaxed and serene.

"And well, she had sneaked this pack of Kools from her mother and umm, we each smoked . . . a couple. Oh, Mom, I know I'm not allowed to smoke, but I thought one wouldn't hurt. I didn't mean to start the second; they didn't taste that good anyhow."

"How do you feel?"

"Pretty awful. I've been throwing up all afternoon. Am I going to get lung cancer?"

I'm smiling, holding back the relieved laughter. "No," I say, "not from two cigarettes."

"Ah, Mom, I'm so sorry."

I'm touched, proud, that she would call to confess.

"So I guess I'm gonna get it when you come home." Her voice is quaking.

"Yes," I answer in my firmest tone, distracted by the memory of Marie's dazzling smile ten minutes before. "I'll have to think of the proper discipline."

"Yes, Mom." She's crying.

I warm up. "It's good that you phoned. Very good. That was the right thing."

"Thanks, Mom." The words are a little quavery, from fear or nausea, I can't tell.

"Drink some bubbly water and walk around the block a couple of times to clear your head," I advise. "A bath might feel nice."

On the bus home, I'm thinking: my world couldn't get much better. Well, there is the matter of moving to our own place far from Mrs. Witch and her kids. But here I am, with two children who trust me, a kind, sexy lover with a quirky sense of humor, and a boss who thinks I'm an artist. What more could I want? A triple crown every few weeks; now that would make life just about perfect.

Grudge Wright

And this is where my naive mistakes began. I had money and time, which turns out to be a dangerous combination for a fledgling comedian with zero anecdotes in his repertoire. I had time, money, two free motel ink pens, and an endless supply of Mankiller's Motor Court memo pads. What did I know?

I sat in the motel room, or down at the Throw Park where all the stray dogs have disappeared, and tried my best not to think like this:

Jumper cable walks into a bar. The bartender says, "Man, you look horrible." The jumper cable says, "Don't get me started."

A sixteen-penny nail walks into a bar and the bartender says, "Can't serve you. You're already hammered."

A right-wing radio personality walks into a bar. The bartender says, "Can I get you anything?" and the guy says, "No thanks, I'm already really fucked up."

A hairbrush walks into a bar. The bartender says, "Hold on, buddy. Don't bristle up on me."

You've heard them all, I'm sure. People always wonder, where do jokes come from? Answer: Me. When I got heckled—nightly—some genius in the audience would always yell out, "Hey, Bazooka Joe, vaudeville's calling and it wants its act back." I didn't care. It was my shtick, as they say. Even people in Winesburg can have a shtick. Some comedians had woeful childhood stories, some stuck to tales of a horrific marriage, some did prop comedy. One guy wore a bag over his head and went by the Unknown Comic, from what I've gathered. Me, I had my *Blank Goes into a Bar:*

A tongue depressor walks into a bar and the bartender says, "Get out of here. You make me gag."

A blow-up rubber sex doll walks into a bar. The bartender says, "What'll you have?" and the sex doll pauses before saying, "It was just on the tip of my tongue. Well, *fuck me.*"

A pair of pliers walks into a bar, but the bartender says, "We don't serve tools."

A screwdriver walks into a bar and orders a vodka and orange juice. The bartender says, "What are you, a cannibal or something?"

Some confetti walks into a bar and the bartender says, "I can't serve you seeing as you're already torn up."

A rectal thermometer walks into a gay bar and gets a hero's welcome.

Nine million, nine hundred ninety-nine thousand, nine hundred ninety-nine lottery tickets walk into a bar. The bartender says, "Sorry, we don't serve such losers."

A rasp walks into a bar and asks the bartender, "Can I drink here if I promise not to grate on your nerves?"

An air horn walks into a bar and the bartender says, "If you're intent on blowing, follow the rectal thermometer next door to the gay bar."

A bipolar woman walks into a bar, but the bartender says, "Last time you were here you split without paying."

An atom walks into a bar and the bartender says, "Last time you were here you split without paying, and all hell broke loose soon thereafter."

A candelabra walks into a bar and the bartender says, "Can't serve anyone already lit."

I bought loaves of white bread, some lunch meat, peanut butter, and wrote my jokes. I drowned out the senior citizen bikers who congregated nightly at the fire pit. I chewed beef jerky, seeing as that seemed a proper thing to do. My motel television didn't have but two clear channels, but I intentionally kept it on channel 2½, all snow, to keep me focused on what would be my nightly routine:

A linebacker walks into a bar. "Hey, don't rush me," says the bartender.

A bowling ball walks into a bar. He says, "I'd like a pint of Mad Dog 20/20." The bartender says, "You can drink better wine than that. You're not in the gutter anymore."

A bowling pin walks into a bar. He says to the bartender, "I'm thirsty, and I don't have any money." The bartender says, "Spare me."

A spigot walks into a bar and asks, "What do you have on tap?"

A spigot walks into a bar. The bartender says, "Sorry, but we don't serve drips."

A ceiling fan walks into a bar. The bartender says, "Draft?"

A blood drive nurse walks into a bar. The bartender says, "You want another pint this soon?"

A rabies victim walks into a bar. The bartender says, "I guess you're ready for another shot in your stomach."

A revolving door walks into a bar. The bartender shakes his head and says, "Turn around."

A bottle of whiteout comes into a bar. "I can't serve your type," says the bartender. "Disappear, buddy."

A chunk of fresco walks into a bar. The bartender says, "Can't serve you. You're plastered."

An ATM machine walks into a bar and orders drinks for everyone. The bartender says, "What are you, like, made of money?"

A length of bubble wrap walks into a bar. The bartender says, "I'm going to keep a close watch on you. Don't pop off."

A champagne cork walks into a bar. The bartender says, "I'm going to keep a close watch on you. Don't pop off."

Carbon paper walks into a bar. The bartender says, "I guess you'll be wanting an Old Fashioned."

A typewriter walks into a bar. The bartender says, "I guess you'll be wanting an Old Fashioned."

Dr. Kevorkian walks into a bar with a little Chinese boy. The bartender says, "We don't serve youth in Asia."

I got six hundred of them. I cannot stop, I know. Where would I go to talk to someone about getting it to stop? Maybe Bloomington. Maybe Indianapolis. I hear there are people in Indianapolis who want to officially change the name of the city to Nativeamericanapolis. I'm betting those people don't have much sense of humor.

People say that you have to live in a sad area in order to come up with funny two-liners. I don't know about that. I've never read an official study. I'm not sure that there are any official studies, here in Winesburg.

Occupy Winesburg

DAY 1

I pitched my tent between the soccer field and the playground in Emile Durkheim Park, across the street from Emile Durkheim High School, my stinking alma mater, and I dove the dumpster at Dollar General for sheets of cardboard. My mother texted: *you're making a fool of yourself, honey.*

Did I care? Hannah Arendt made a fool of herself. Rosa Parks, too. Fucking Gandhi was the biggest fool of them all. I chuckled at public humiliation. I was the sole Occupier in Winesburg; alone in the park. The movement was me; I was the movement.

When I saw the principal of Durkheim High coming down the block in her minivan, I hustled into my tent for the sign I'd made just for her. *I Reject Your Authority as Illegitimate.* She shrugged at me benignly as she drove past my encampment, on her way to indoctrinate the current generation of Winesburg youth in capitalism and civic complacency. With one hand I held my sign high, and with the other hand I flipped her the bird.

Don't kid yourself that Winesburg is a haven from corporate America. Don't go thinking this town is special because a few mom & pops—the meat store, the funeral home—have so far survived the global economic meltdown. Don't go thinking that the people here have some sort of community ethic about preserving small-town culture. The parking lot of the Target on Highway 8 last holiday season? Mayhem. Emile Durkheim's grand theories of cultural interdependence and organic solidarity trampled under the boots of Black Friday shoppers.

What they didn't teach you at EDHS, by the way, was anything about Durkheim himself, the father of modern sociology. I needed big cardboard real estate to quote him in full. I raided the dumpster at Winesburg Appliance. They were under new local management, claimed the sign, but hardly anybody knew they'd actually gotten bought out by Whirlpool. I found a refrigerator box. *If society lacks the unity based upon the commitment of men's wills to a common objective,* I lettered artfully in purple Sharpie, *then it is no more than a pile of sand that the least jolt or the slightest puff will suffice to scatter.* I poked holes in the corners of the Durkheim quote and strung my sign between the swing set and the maple tree under which Bobby McReynolds had once kissed me before he went away to college.

DAY 5

My mother came by the encampment with tuna sandwiches and a Diet Coke. I was pretty hungry, so I tolerated her sighs and groans as she crawled into my tent. "Remember the summer we went to Yosemite?" she said. "Remember that bear?"

I dug into the tuna. I love my mother's tuna. She makes it with sweet relish and mustard. She examined my sleeping bag, my plastic tub of clothes and books, organized and ready for a bug-out in case I was evicted in the middle of the night. There wasn't a whole lot to do out here. I couldn't even catch the wi-fi signal from the high school. Mostly I waited around for the cops to come tell me I couldn't camp in the park. I was hungry for an arrest. Something.

"What's the deal here, honey?" my mother said. "I mean, what's the point?"

My mother had double-mortgaged her home to cover my father's hospital bills, for all the good that did us: he died anyhow, not a dime of life insurance. Now her home, the home where I grew up, was in foreclosure. Ditto two other houses on our block, and three on the next street. No college fund for yours truly, either. And here my mother sat, asking me what's the point. Winesburg, Indiana: not really so special.

DAY 12

On Wall Street and in Oakland they were drumming and teaching-in and taking pepper spray in the face. I thumb-typed a Declaration of Principles on my cell phone. I started a Facebook page. I educated myself in horizontal structures and direct democracy. I was ready to facilitate a General Assembly, as soon as there were others to assemble. But I was tired of waiting around for Winesburgers to wake up to the reality of a ruined world. I zipped up my tent and went to the Target on Highway 8. My sign said *Everything is Okay, Just Keep Shopping.*

My mom came out of the store, pushing one of those oversized red carts. "Well, hi there, honey," she said. She rummaged around in the plastic bags and handed me a box of Little Debbie's Devil Squares. My dad used to love those things. "I've been thinking," she said, waving her fingers to indicate my sign, my worldview, my involvement in the coming revolution. "Whatever makes you happy is okay with me."

Emile Durkheim wrote that through collective consciousness, people become aware of one another as social beings, and that we produce collective consciousness through our interactions with one another. This strikes me as obvious. But you get the sense that he was quite the radical thinker for his time. Or maybe it was obvious all along. Maybe Emile was just saying what people always knew in their hearts to be true.

I watched my mom push the cart back to her car, across the asphalt expanse. The Target security guard came out of the store and told me I couldn't stand there. Then he said, "Hey. Your dad was my soccer coach."

I didn't remember him. His name tag said Elmer, but I was pretty sure that wasn't his name. You don't forget a name like Elmer. My dad loved those soccer boys. He coached that team for ten years, talked like every last one of his players was some sort of miracle, special in a profound way. Even the klutzes. I said, "What will you do if I don't leave?"

Elmer lit a cigarette and seemed to think about it. He thought for a good long while, smoking and watching customers come and go. "He was a good coach," Elmer said at last. "I'm sorry about what happened." He stepped on his cigarette and then went back inside.

I opened the box of Little Debbies. They reminded me of course of my father, which made me really fucking sad, so there I was holding my sign and stuffing my face with Devil Squares and crying in front of the Target. Which isn't exactly the ideal way to change the world.

I took the bus to the Bank of America branch on Maple Grove and attached myself by the neck to the front door with a U-shaped bicycle lock. It was super uncomfortable, let me tell you. The handle was at an awkward height, forcing me to sort of crouch there, unable to sit or stand. Plus the lock was pressing fairly hard against my windpipe.

The security guard came outside, and I thought, all right, here we go. But he was followed by the manager, Dave, a wiry guy with big feet who used to be on my dad's bowling team. I'd forgotten Dave worked there. His daughter, Julie, and I used to sip Cokes at the bowling alley's shoe rental counter while we waited for our dads to finish their games. Which they cheerfully lost, pretty much every week.

Dave sipped at his cup of coffee, sized up the situation. "Hey there, Suzie," he said. "What's cooking?"

"You fuckers foreclosed on my mom's house," I croaked. I didn't like calling him that, because it was always Dave who had quarters in his pocket for the Coke machine. But honestly: there's a global economic meltdown in progress, and actual human beings are in pain.

"Oh, that," he said. "Right." He gestured to the security guard and the guy went away. While I waited for whatever was going to happen next, I informed Dave about Emile Durkheim's thoughts on the cultural aspect of the collective consciousness. "We're emotionally bound to culture," I told him. "The emotional part of the collective consciousness overrides our egoism. We act socially because we recognize it's the responsible, moral way to act."

"You don't say," Dave replied.

The security guard appeared, carrying an enormous pair of bolt cutters. He placed them tenderly between my neck and the door handle and with a little grunt he snapped the U-lock and I was freed.

Dave laid a hand on my shoulder. "You know what, sweetheart? I don't mind saying this. Your dad would've been proud of your spunk."

"Have a nice day," the security guard told me.

DAY 23

I was at my mom's house, packing up my old stuffed animals and Brainiac trophies when Larry from AAAA Locksmith came to the door. "Gotta do this," he told my mom. "Sorry."

"You're early!" she wailed. She waved a letter from the bank. "I have two more days! The freezer is full of meat!"

Larry examined the letter. He pointed out a sentence containing the words "may" and "at the discretion of" and "up to 7 days before your foreclosure date." I snatched the letter from his hand and climbed to my roof. The day before, I had decamped from the park and reinstalled myself on the roof of the house. The pitch of the roof made it pretty hard to sleep, but I'd weighted the tent down with foreclosed paving bricks I liberated from the foreclosed patio. I'd lettered *Emile Durkheim Forever* in Sharpie on a pillowcase flag and flew it from the chimney. I painted STOLEN AMERICAN DREAM across the shingles in big block letters of pink latex paint still sitting around from when my dad built my playhouse.

I waved the letter from Bank of America, and translated for the neighbors, who had begun to congregate on their lawns, the sentence that authorized Larry to change the locks on my mother's house. "We are the bank and we are legally entitled to screw you," I yelled, "for as long and as hard as we damn well please!" My voice was hoarse. I'd been yelling quite a lot from the roof in the past week, to tell you the truth. The neighbors had been tolerant about it—my dad had been a popular guy, the kind of man who'd shovel your walk when you're out of town to confuse the burglars—but I'm guessing they weren't so disappointed to see Larry the Locksmith. They were tired of watching our misfortune, tired of thinking how close they were, too, to falling into this well of bad luck.

"Shame!" I yelled at Larry, who really was just some guy trying to make a living. I wasn't being fair, but none of this was fair.

A cruiser from the Winesburg Police Department showed up. The cops conferred with Larry at the front door, blocking the entrance to our home. My mother stood in our driveway in her house slippers and sweatpants and wept. Our neighbor Irene held her by the shoulders, tried to steer her inside, then seemed to realize my mother no longer had an inside to be steered toward. By now, everyone was on their front porches, on the sidewalks. Kids on bikes circled around the street. "Shame!" I yelled at the sky. "Shame on everyone!"

Constance Wootin, the ancient crazy artist lady who lives at the end of the block, appeared at the edge of the crowd, leaning on the arm of a young man who turned out to be Bobby McReynolds, home from college. Bobby was carrying a bright green duffel bag and an aluminum folding chair. They made their slow way into our yard, Constance ignoring the cops and the neighbors and the general tumult. She pointed to a spot on the grass, unfolded the chair, and settled herself. Bobby gave me a little salute, unzipped the duffel bag, and like a magic trick out popped an orange tent. A little backpacking tent, just big enough for two. The neighbors surged forward for a look. Constance reached into a tote bag covered with splotches of paint and pulled out a brush and a palette and painted OCCUPY WINESBURG right on the nylon.

Everyone stood around muttering energetically as they watched Constance and her slow paintbrush. When she finished and stood up, it was as though she'd startled a flock of birds. The neighbors dashed away. From my vantage point on my roof I watched them opening their garages and storage sheds, rooting around inside. Kids biked in tight circles around the locksmith's truck, making war whoops.

Within twenty minutes, our neighbors' tents overflowed the lawn, spilled onto the sidewalk, filled the street. Kids struggled with poles. Dads pounded stakes into our grass. Somebody brought coffee and cookies.

My mother clapped and clapped. She bounced on her toes. She pushed past the cops and went inside. She came back out with the American flag my father had flown on holidays, inserted it into the brace on the front porch.

She stepped back, shaded her eyes, and found me on the roof, where I was sitting with my legs dangling over the edge. Bobby McReynolds had climbed up and was grinning at my side. Our yard was a bright fluttering sea of blues and yellows and greens.

We weren't idiots. We knew that this was all too late, that the house was already lost, that these tents would be cleared out tomorrow, that my father was dead and gone. But when my mother raised the flag, it felt, for a moment, like we were still living in the America we once knew.

The Cantor Quadruplets

The town donated a house to us. It came with a town-donated trailer out back, back in the corner of the lot, its tires shot, hitch rusted out, propane cans empty empty. The used trailer was another donation to us, to the local miracle of us, along with a lifetime supply of diapers, another lifetime supply of formula, another lifetime supply of car seats, and a gross of pacifiers. We thought our folks thought that, one day, fixed up, we'd all haul the whole wreck over some horizon, the hole wreck of us, get the smell out of Dodge at least for a weak-end. Go to *The Lake*. Skate. Rent space in the gravelscape of an overgrown KIA. Any place other than the here-and-now that more and more was looking like the here-and-ever-after-after. After the old man split for some seener pastures, Mom, she started holing up in that tin can. "Me time," she called it. "You kids," she'd swell, "stay in the goddamn yard." She drank Cutty from Dixie cups, fond, she was, of the green bottle's picture, a sad ship reaching on some tactless tack, and sifted through slick magazines and the old joyless *Joy of Looking,* ripping out pages of recipes for stews and ragouts she never made, finding the find print too fine. Starting. Starting lists. Starting lists of ingredients. We ate out of cans. We saw her through the hatches and holes as we ran past, red-rovering, crack-the-whipping, staying staying in the yard. At night, no light. We hunted down lumbering lightning bugs, crushed them out like cigarettes in our palms, their butt ash throbbing the there there there there. In that dark, she trailed out of the trailer, climbed the latter to the heap's hump roof like she was climbing out from under underwater to float on the surface of a silver pool and Mom mom-bathe in the mooning moonlight, one big refracting reflection, shadows bouncing around, dodge balls getting out of Dodge. The yard shingled with the shells of sucked-dry Pet Milk cans breached with the beak of a chirp key, and all of us us-es, staying in the goddamn yard, staying frozen in this freeze tag till this lifetime supply of Hell's Hell freezes over.

Reverend Dave

For a time, life in Winesburg was good, and the Lord Our God blessed our town with prosperous yields, fertile soil, and faithful Christian soldiers. My flock was rapidly expanding, the pews in First Family of Christ Living Center and Day Care overflowing with spirits in desperate need of saving.

I was happy to oblige.

"I will show you the One Way," I bellowed from the pulpit. "I will lead you to the glorious land of salvation."

In addition to Sunday service, I also held Ladies' Night each Thursday, during which I offered a similar message, though slightly altered to appeal to the female audience.

"Rise up and lower yourself for His Humble Servant, the Reverend Dave," I preached, "and I will make my deposit into your temple!"

Some of the more God-fearing women were skeptical of my advances, though I assured them the Lord smiled upon those whose passions knew no bounds.

"But . . . is promiscuity not a sin, Reverend?" inquired the buxom Jackie Patch, to which I pressed a firm hand to her left buttock and replied, "My sweet lamb, the commingling of sacred temples is a blessing to God."

That very night she and I blessed Him several times, glory to God in the highest.

✳   ✳   ✳

There are two types of laws in Winesburg—man's law and God's—and while I left Sheriff Gordon to dole out the former, I took much care in doling out the latter. There was never any doubt whether or not a car was double-parked, though the great moral questions required interpretation, and I was the town's sole interpreter. For years, the Lord rewarded my interpretations by bestowing upon me an entire cornucopia of Winesburg's most eligible bachelorettes, and, never one to shy away from the Lord's generosity, I helped myself to His bounty on a nightly basis.

And then one night—prior to commingling with a young, thick-thighed maid by the name of Bridgette Steepleton—the contemptible Pastor John infected our quiet town with his heresy. He was a bicep-laden, square-chinned Pentecostal from the sinful city of Fort Wayne; worse still, he had no qualms about storming into the only lit building in town on Thursday night—Emile Durkheim High School—and interrupting the PTA meeting to make his presence known.

"Something is rotten in the state of Winesburg," Pastor John informed the Parent-Teacher Association—a literary reference lost on all but English teacher Ms. Lydia Hatcher, who began clapping wildly from her place in the second row.

"Point of clarification," corrected PTA secretary Joseph Lowry, licking the tip of his pencil. "According to the zoning board, Winesburg is classified as a town, not a state. I'll make a clarifying note in the minutes."

"Duly noted," Pastor John humbly agreed before starting in on his true purpose—publicly decrying the town's spiritual leader (me) for having taken part in what he deemed "improper relations" with many of the "fertile, young lambs" of the congregation.

I, an at-large member of the PTA (a post I regretted as soon as I realized childless bachelorettes didn't attend PTA meetings), cloaked myself in God's protective graces by faking sleep, resting my head against my chest and snoring at a pitch just loud enough to assure the other PTA members that my lack of rebuttal was due to the exhaustion of their overworked reverend and not a sign of weakness. I tried to deduce exactly what had brought this cretin to our town, but the possibilities were endless.

Had I helped myself to a few handfuls of his congregation's tithes during my stint as a traveling preacher?

Had I imbibed too deeply from the blood of Christ he'd offered?

My sins—while modest—were far-reaching.

"I challenge Reverend Dave to a faith-off," Pastor John continued, interrupting my speculation. "Tomorrow evening, in this very auditorium, I will stand before you and perform the five signs as indicated in the book of Mark. I shall cast out devils, speak in tongues, take up serpents, drink deadly things, and lay my hands on the sick to heal them."

In a matter of moments, the PTA meeting had become far more interesting than the association ever imagined, and quite suddenly, voting for the approval of a new fleet of pencil sharpeners no longer seemed a priority.

"I know not where your so-called reverend is hiding," Pastor John began as several heads turned in my direction, "but make him aware of my challenge. Tomorrow evening, come prepared to witness miracles performed by the truly faithful."

With that, the forked-tongued pastor swept across the gymnasium floor and allowed the PTA meeting to continue precisely where it had left off.

"Very well then. Any new business?" asked PTA president Donald Crumble.

There was none.

"Motion to adjourn?"

The motion was seconded.

The association scuttled into the hallway to partake in punch and cookies, at which point I, the town's spiritual leader and at-large PTA member, snapped awake and quite heroically snuck out the emergency exit door.

❋   ❋   ❋

The following afternoon, as Pastor John spiritually prepared himself for the miracles ahead—anointing his body with rosemary-scented oil just beneath the basketball hoop of the Emile Durkheim High School gymnasium—I watched on from a cracked door in a nearby janitorial supply closet. What I witnessed was nothing short of shocking—a man seemingly in complete control of his faith. He appeared somehow exempt from the world's temptations. I sent the ferociously beautiful Helen Koppelford (Emile Durkheim's head cheerleader) into his recently anointed arms offering leftover punch and cookies from the PTA meeting, and he refused her kindly, sending her on her way without casting so much as a lustful eye.

As she walked away, Helen spied me from my place within the closet and shrugged, as if she too could not understand a man whose faith was not the least bit shaken by the great depths of her low-cut halter.

✳   ✳   ✳

Hours later, when Pastor John left to relieve himself in the boys' room, I leapt from the janitor's closet, returning home to begin my own spiritual preparation—two Advil and a whiskey sour. As the clock struck seven, I gathered my suitcase of faith-healing tools and set off toward the high school. The school's doors were flung wide, and a carnival atmosphere had developed, my once-faithful flock now anxiously awaiting my trial.

I placed my suitcase beside a chair facing the audience, while alongside me Pastor John had his own tools—a chicken-wire crate full of coiling rattlesnakes as well as vials of strychnine.

The crowd took their seats as Pastor John approached me, held out a leathery hand, and whispered, "So you're the lecherous old codger who knocked up my niece, eh?"

I stared at him, foggily recalling a feisty, red-headed vixen with the same square chin, the same Pentecostal upbringing. She was a young lamb whose temple I'd breached on several occasions, glory to God in the highest. However, I hadn't been aware that my Essence played a role in her child's not-so-immaculate conception.

"Perhaps this was God's will," I began, stuttering. "Glory to God in the . . ."

"God's will," he scoffed, fiddling with his snake box. "Allow me to show you God's will."

And then, with the precision of a skilled mountebank, Pastor John proceeded to cast out devils, blather in tongues, slurp down strychnine, lay his hands on Henry Compton (a longtime sufferer of whooping cough), and drape an entire knot of rattlesnakes upon his sweaty head. My flock watched on in wonderment, praising the Lord for bringing this righteous man to their humble town.

"Hallelujah!" they cried. "Praise Him!"

Impressed with himself (though I will remind you pride is a sin), Pastor John returned the snakes to their box before offering an extended bow as the crowd erupted in cheers, overcome by the power of the Lord.

Pastor John returned to his chair while every eye in the room shifted toward me, creating a silence louder than the tumbling walls of Jericho.

"My loyal flock," I cried, beginning my reverend stroll across the length of the gym floor. "Before being swayed by such vapid parlor tricks, allow me to show you the One Way. Allow me to lead you to the glorious land of . . . salvation!"

I had hoped words alone might reaffirm my place as Winesburg's spiritual leader, though a few of the men crossed their arms, assuring me that they required miracles.

"Well all right, then," I said, stammering, "to begin, allow me to . . . cast out a devil."

I turned to Pastor John, arms outstretched, and shouted, "Scat, devil! Git a move on, you serpentine scoundrel!"

I made a few kicks at the air while Pastor John helped himself to a sip of water.

"Very well then," I continued, unlatching my suitcase. "On to miracle number two."

I pulled out my abridged Latin dictionary and began reciting languages in tongues foreign to the ears of Winesburg, though when that, too, failed to impress, I took a full swallow of the day-old punch from the PTA meeting, which was pretty lethal in itself. A few of my faithful were already heading toward the exits, so I upped the ante, offering Henry Compton a spoonful of Robitussin to soothe his throat before concluding by pulling two writhing garter snakes from my suitcase and thrusting them toward heaven.

When I fell to my knees shouting, "Glory to God in the highest!" a single clap echoed off the cinder block walls.

As that clap dissipated, it became suddenly clear that my services were no longer needed; that all my canoodling and commingling had backfired, that somewhere along my path to saving souls I had, perhaps, desecrated one too many temples.

Shoulders slumped, I collected my suitcase and headed toward the door.

But I'd yet to reach that door when God blessed me with a miracle, indeed!

Upon hearing a gasp from the crowd, I turned to find Pastor John toppled to the floor, collapsed in a heap on the free throw line. The strychnine was proving too powerful—even for a man of his faith—and the people of Winesburg turned once more to their spiritual rock (me) to save that wicked pastor from death's greedy embrace.

"My children," I shouted, leaping into action, "we must pray for a doctor! We must pray for this terribly sinful man to receive the medical attention he requires!"

We clasped our hands tight as Dr. Grover Rayburn—a longtime member of the congregation—walked unsteadily toward the sick man, his cane clicking, and pronounced the pastor "still alive."

"But he ought not to have drank up all that poison like a damn fool," Rayburn diagnosed. "If he was smart he'd vomit it right back up."

Quite heroically (and with the Lord's strength), I lifted John's sweaty head into my arms and forced him to drink what remained of the day-old PTA punch. Almost immediately, the poison came flooding out of his mouth like a red sea and the congregation cheered my miracle—claiming it the truest display of spiritual healing they'd ever witnessed.

"I am no hero," I proclaimed modestly as Pastor John continued retching beneath the basketball net, "for the Lord God has blessed me with great strength and fortitude and—"

"Rattlesnakes! Goddamn!" a voice cried out, and I turned to observe the last of the snakes slithering from their unlatched cage and winding around the wood-paneled floor. God spoke to me then—a voice I hadn't heard in years—whispering, "Dave, this moment calls for divine leadership." And then it struck me: this moment, quite simply, called for Reverend Dave.

Like Moses on Sinai, like Christ on the Mount, I climbed to the high ground, leaping heroically to the top of the bleachers. While some of the more brazen men tested their own faith to recapture those snakes, I stood atop the bleachers and prayed for their wives, promising the Lord Our God that if, heaven forbid, anything were to befall those gentle souls, I might offer their wives sanctuary on all the coldest and loneliest nights.

Professor Helen C. Andersen

The new fabulist moved into her office this week. It is next to my office. I asked my chair to assign her an office on the other end of the building, because I am a very private person, but he assigned her the office next to mine. My chair claims I will be a good mentor for her. He put in a one-way mirror between us so she could observe me. But why would I be a good mentor for her? She has streaky blonde hair with pale pink highlights; she wears three-inch heels and straight-legged jeans. Why would she need mentoring from me? Let's be realistic here. I have lived in this town for my entire forty-three years and wear my grandmother's clothes. I am not a good mentor for her. I can see that she judges my outfits by the way she watches me through her side of the mirror. My life was nice before. It was quiet. I did all my research at the town library, where my daughter is the librarian. There is a desk in the children's room always waiting for me. But then I was asked to keep watch over her. Why? She showed up in town with her pink and blonde hair and her new collection of stories about flying ponies, and everyone loved her on sight. But I'm dutiful. I know my place. I started going to my office at school more often—in order to mentor her, of course. If I am asked to do something I do it. I am a realist that way. And one must help the town's newest women fit in . . . it isn't easy. The women in this town can be cold. My other daughter was a real victim of them. How do you stay so thin, I asked the new one over lunch just today, in an effort to mentor her. Is it natural, or do you have a problem? I asked her. People in town may start to think you have a problem, I told her, if you do not gain weight. As for me, I have problems. (This is just between us.) One of my problems, it seems, is that when I sit down to write, I do not write about flying pink ponies. My stories do not come to me through telepathy, as the new fabulist says her stories do come to her. They appear on my forehead and I read them in the mirror, she told me, her eyes brimming with tears in an effort to manipulate me. As for me, I have a very large forehead and I fear it makes me look like a man. My new project is to find out things about her to expose her as the fraud that she really is. For example, did you know that she was once hospitalized for attempted suicide? If nothing else, I will always have that. I mean who does she think she is? I've had enough of that with my daughters. And pink ponies. Pink hair. This town was a lot nicer before her arrival, before she came here. Now, when I look in the mirror, there is a terrible glare. She's on the other side of it—always—I fear.

Inspector 4

I am in quality control. I am quality control. I control quality here at the Pink Pearl factory. My job is to write out something, anything, on this piece of paper, and, then, test the eraser, a random nub from the lot, and erase, erasing every word. So, I use my test, this simulation, to write to you. I write this to you who worry that there will be evidence, a record, of our secret. "I just don't want anybody hurt," you write to me. "Destroy this," you write at the end of the note where you wrote "I just don't want anybody hurt." I'm an expert, making language disappear. No more phone calls. "Your number will show up on the bill," you say when you call. "Strike me," you whisper, "from the call log on your phone." I control quality. I am qualified. I make space. Gaps. I erase erasures. "We must," you say, "not get carried away," "Delete 'Delete.'" "You are driving me crazy," you write in the e-mail, my e-mail dangling down below where I have typed that you drive me crazy not from what you write but the way you hold my head, your fingers rubbing through my hair, how I spread open your lips with my tongue, its tip touching that nub, your pink pearl, sanding it flat, the stubble of my beard, iridescent irritant. "Rubbed raw," I write. Abrasion. My hand in your mouth. You gagged silent. No one should know any of this. Ever. We must control ourselves. Not write down anything. No evidence. Forget even this. Nothing left but some crumbs rubbed clean, brushed from the empty, empty, empty, empty paper.

I am in   control. I   control. I control   here
   the Pink Pearl   write out something, anything, on this piece   ,   test the eraser, a random
nub   erase, erasing every word.   my test,
this simulation, to write to you. I write this to you who worry
there will be evidence, a record,   our secret. "I just don't want
          hurt," you write to me. "Destroy this," you write at the
end   you wrote "I just don't want   hurt."
I'm   making language disappear. No   phone calls.
"Your number will show up   ," you say when   .
"Strike me," you whisper, "from the call   I control   I make space. Gaps. I erase erasures.
"We must," you say, "   get carried away," "Delete 'Delete.'" "
   driving me crazy," you write   dangling
down below where I have typed   you
   you write   the way you hold my head, your fingers rubbin
through my hair,   I spread   your lips   my tongue, its
tip touching that nub, your pink pearl, sand   it flat, the stubble
   , iridescent irritant. "Rubb   raw," I write. Abrasion.
My hand in your mouth.   gagged silent. No one   know
any of this. Ever. We   control ourselves.   write down
          evidence. Forget even this. Nothing left   some
crumbs rubbe   clean, brush   from the empty, empty,   ,
empty paper.

I   m in   control. I   c nt   . c nt   here
    the Pink Pearl   write out   me   , any-
    i   ,   this piece   ,   test the eraser,   random
nub   erase, eras   every wo .   my test,
    is simulation, to   rite   you. I rite   you   worry
there will be   our secret. "I just   want
            hurt,"   me. Destroy this   at the
end   I just   want
I'm   making language disappear. No
"Your   will show up   you say   .
    Strike me   you whisper,   call   I con-
trol   I make   Gaps. erase erasures.
    We must   get carried away   "Delete 'Delete.'" "
          me crazy," you   dangling
down below where I   typed   you
        you   the way you hold my head,   fingers rubbi
through   hair,   I spread   lips   my tongue,
tip touch   that nub, your pink pearl, sand   it flat, the stub
                    scent irritant. Rub   raw   I   it   Abrasion.
    hand in   mouth.   gag   silent. No one   now
any of this. Ever. We   rol ourselves.   writ do
                evidence. Forget   this Nothing   some
crumbs rubbe   clean, b ush   o   the   , empty,   ,
empty paper.

in   c nt   . I   c nt   . c nt   here

Pink Pearl   rite   me   , an

i ,   this pie   ,   the eraser,   random

nu   erase, era   eve   wo .   test,

is simulation, to   you. I   you   worry

there will   our secret.   just   want

me.   Destroy   the

end   I just   want

language disappear. No   .

You   will show up   you   .

Strike me   you whisper,   call   I con-

trol   I make   Gaps.   erase   sure .

We must   get   away   'Delete.'" "

me   you   dangling

below   I   typed   you

you   the   you hold my head,   fingers rub

rough   air,   I   re d   lips   tongue,

tip touch   that   ink pearl, sand   it   at,   stub

scent irritant. Rub   aw   I   it   ion.

hand in   mouth.   gag   silent. No on   now

this. Ever. We   our   .   it   do

id   Forget   Nothing   o

crumbs rub   lean,   us   o   , empty,   ,

paper.

```
     in                .I                         .                        here
        Pink Pearl                         it          me         , an
   i   ,     is  i              ,                    the erase ,    and
                        erase,          eve          .                      test,
                on,            you. I                    you
   the     will                          our secret.       us            want
                                  me.                                       the
   end                       I  us       want
                             disappear. No                               .
   You              will show                  you                         .
         me   you           ,              call                    I
                        make                        erase
      us                             away           '   let .'" "
             me          you
         below       I                   you
      you              you       my              fingers rub
               air,      I                               tongue,
   tip              at              pearl,
                        irritant.              I     it        i  .
      and i          out  .     gag    i   .  o o              now
         this.     . We               o          .          it  do
                        get           Nothing              o
         rub            us      o              , empty,           ,
         paper.
```

.　　　　　　　.

Pink Pearl　　　　　　　　　me　　　,

,　　　　　　　,　　　　　erase ,

　　erase,　　　　　　.　　　　test,

　　you.　　　　you

　　　　our secret.　us

　　　　.

　　　　disappear.　　　　.

　　show　　　　　　.

me　you　　　,　　　　　　I

　　　　　　erase

us　　　　　away　　'　　.'" "

　me　　you

　　　　you

you　　　you　　　　rub

　air,　I

　　　pearl

　　irritant.　　　.

　out　　　　.

is.　.　　　o　.　　o

　　　o　　　o

rub　　o　　, empty,　,

paper.

.   .

                                                    ,

,   ,   erase ,

            erase,   .

                    .

                        secret.

                .

                    disappear.   .

        show   .

            ,

                                    erase

                        away   '   .'" "

                                                    rub

    ,   I

                    pearl

                .   .

        out   .

    .   .   o   .   o

                                        o   o

    rub   o   , empty,   ,

paper.

Dark Stars

Those two pit bulls playing out on the street belong to that pink house right across from mine. A mother, son, and daughter live there too, more ink on their six fat arms than the bumper Sunday paper. I don't want to think about what they might have put over the rest of themselves. No, I'm not judging people by their cover. I got a tattoo, my very own constellation of stars. The most stars that could fit onto the back of my little neck. I always was skinny. Bones like a fish, some men said. Bones, my first husband said, that he could pick from between his teeth. I never did feel there was enough of me, especially not after all he took out of me.

I don't have ink anywhere else and only a handful of people ever saw that one tat under this veil of hair, hair black and warm as this cardigan once. My father hated tattoos, said they defaced God's work. Ever we meet in the next life, I'm going to tell him that men did more to deface me inside and out than any tattoo—

Oh, I'm laughing because I'm remembering I *was* like a fish. So hard to grasp and then slip away.

Feels good to laugh. I laugh often as I can.

'Course, fish don't always get away.

They tubby too, those three in the pink house, with greasy hair, flat faces, and eyebrows that look Sharpied on. Got those pit bulls as pups, but the beasts have grown. Huge! A hundred pounds apiece, if you're going to ask specifics, and chests wide and white and solid. Owners let those dogs run without leashes and both animals full stop with a scratch of nails whenever I come out my front door. Dogs seem to smile, soft and kind, like they want to play, but I knew several men that smiled like that in the beginning. It's always worse after you been hurt bad in body and mind, you know what can come again. Some days I can't get outside at all on account of those dogs. I know those dogs be well loved and looked after. They be happy, too, be playing, laughing, wagging their whole selves. But all beasts be unpredictable. Loaded.

I'm gonna call animal control, just as soon as I can figure out how to do so nonamously. Nights, I can't sleep thinking about those dogs tearing me apart, going for my soft throat, shaking what's left of my insides out onto the pavement. Then there's my 'mares about the mother, son, and daughter finding out I done reported the dogs and coming after me with baseball bats. Beating me to stew in time to a chant I can't even hear anymore. Meanwhile the pit bulls, just sprung from the pound, put on bibs and tighten their paws around knives and forks.

Look! There they are again. See those eyes and teeth, gleaming wet. And those monster paws, bigger than any hand that ever touched me wrong. See the tall point on those ears, could cut through skin with a single twitch. Those damn dogs make the stars want to walk right off of me.

Every now and then, I look at my stars with mirrors. Have to catch up all my hair and angle and wangle, but I manage to see my masterpiece well enough. Watch that faded blue ink inside those strange-limbed shapes, like the night sky done bled into the stars. I should have just inked outlines and left those stars the color of

God's work. But it's as if I experienced some foresight all those years back when I was a young woman and first went under the needle. Like I knew so much would go inside out on me in this world and right where I'd be sure to find light, I wouldn't.

Clyde

Hi, I am Clyde.

About a month ago, I was solicited to write a personal account of my life in Winesburg, Indiana. It's been a tough life, what with the gigantism and all. The person who solicited me goes by the name Bryan Furuness. I know, the name sounds made up. I wrote him back and asked him what I would get paid, and he wrote back and said "nothing."

Bryan works for a magazine called *Booth*. I don't know what that means. There's John Wilkes Booth, who shot the president, and there is the booth you sit in at a diner, and there is the telephone booth. *Booth* magazine? I know, I know, it, too, sounds made up.

As far as I can tell, *Booth* is an "online" magazine. This means it doesn't exist in reality. It has no physical form. It also means that it could disappear in the snap of a fingers. (Perhaps it is already gone?) What this has to say about its editor, Bryan Furuness, I'll leave to your imagination.

But enough about Bryan Furuness. This piece is supposed to be about me, and my tragic life in Winesburg, Indiana. It is a most curious thing, though. When Bryan contacted me about this assignment, he asked that I write a monologue about my life in the fictional town of Winesburg. The *fictional* town of Winesburg. Needless to say, that one word didn't slip by unnoticed. *Fictional*? Who is this invisible person—who works for a paperless magazine—to claim that I don't really exist? To claim that my entire *town* doesn't exist? *Sheesh*! You might as well say Springfield doesn't exist!

I've actually never been to Springfield. I have a weak constitution, which makes traveling an uneasy proposition. But I've seen Springfield on maps. Ms. Crystal brought them out during the unit on Indiana state politics. If I were to leave Winesburg, it would only take a couple hours by car to get to Springfield (and even less by ferry).

Ms. Crystal knew all about the history of Indiana. She knew the names of the five vice presidents who were Hoosiers, including Thomas A. Hendricks (and a lot of people forget him, seeing as he was only in office for a few months). Vice President Hendricks was from nearby Shelbyville. (Just try and tell me that Shelbyville doesn't exist!) Hendricks was Grover Cleveland's vice president, but then he died from swallowing a toothpick. Such was the respect for Thomas A. Hendricks that the position of vice president was left empty until Levi Morton took office—four whole years later! This is all stuff I learned from Ms. Crystal, before I was diagnosed with Alien Hand Syndrome, and before I came down with Parrot Fever.

As you may have noticed, I suffer from a number of ailments. A few years ago my buddy Dale Rumsey suggested I go see Winesburg's preeminent (and only) shrink.

Dale, in case you are wondering (ahem, Mr. Furuness), is more than just my imaginary friend. Just now I went to check out the *Booth* magazine website, and Dale's monologue about his life in Winesburg is already there! You should check it out!

Dale is a good guy. We were in Ms. Crystal's history class together in junior high. Even back then he was obsessed with aliens. Dale is a distant cousin of Leonard Nimoy, twice removed and that sort of thing, and I think he kind of got obsessed with Nimoy, as did I, especially that show *In Search Of . . .* , which was about finding things that supposedly don't exist. Dale himself has never been anally probed, but he has talked to a lot of Winesburgians who have been, including Mrs. Camden, who miscarried her alien baby, and Dale has a collection of alien "scat," which is just a fancy word for "poop," which he wants to put in a museum.

Dale told me I should go visit Dr. Elyria, not because he could cure me, but because you could talk to him for almost a full hour without getting interrupted. Dale and I—and this is going way back to junior high—we never had a lot of folks to talk to. And Dale can't talk to me anymore, on account of my hearing (tinnitus), so that's how he got to seeing Dr. E. Dr. E got his psych degree at Indiana Polytechnic Junior College over there in Terre Haute.

Dr. E has an interesting story. His roommate freshman year at IPJC was none other than Billy Joe Cuthbert. This was back when Billy Joe was displaying the same basketball prowess that would eventually take him to the NBA. As the story goes, Billy Joe was having an existential crisis, and the coach of the Polytechnic Fire-Breathing Chimera came to Dr. E—this was back when Dr. E was an econ major—and asked him to talk to Billy Joe. I guess Dr. E knew his stuff, because Billy got back on the hardwood and went on to have that successful career with the Utah Jazz, and Dr. E switched tracks and found his calling.

Speaking of tracks, I've totally gone off mine. It's probably on account of the brain cleft from which I suffer. Anyway, I did end up going to see Dr. E, and I told him all about my problems, and he said that they didn't exist, and that they were all in my head. "What about the gigantism?" I said, holding up my size nineteen left foot. "Oh, that's real," he admitted.

On the measure of my existence, I can't help but to think I exist. I remember Ms. Crystal teaching us the expression "I think therefore I am." Some famous guy said that. Ms. Crystal was my first crush. She was what the kids these days call a "cougar." Believe me, she existed. Not only did she exist in the classroom on the first floor at Winesburg Junior High—the windowless room that doubled as a tornado shelter—but also in my imagination. In striped bikinis she existed, and in nylon stockings, and swinging by my house in her red Trans Am while my parents were out because she wanted to personally deliver the best student paper about alien probes that she'd ever read.

As it turned out, the best grade Ms. Crystal ever gave me was for a book report I wrote on Leonard Nimoy's autobiography. The book was called *I Am Not Spock.* Some people were upset when this book came out. (Dale, for instance.) They insisted that Leonard Nimoy *was* Spock. Because if Leonard Nimoy *wasn't* Spock, then who *was*? Me? Dale? If no one *was* Spock, then Spock didn't exist! Back then, that proposition was a hard one for some people around here to swallow (me especially, because of the Schatzki's ring I have in my esophagus). Thankfully, Leonard Nimoy followed his first failed autobiography with a second successful one. It was called *I Am Spock.* I didn't read that one, but I suppose he must have changed his mind.

The truth is, sometimes I wish I could say, "I Am Not Clyde." Sometimes, I'd like to be somebody else, somebody who didn't have a giant foot and an alien hand and a bad ear and a constricted esophagus. I'd like to be a Bigfoot detective or an astronaut or Ms. Crystal's gynecologist. But what I am is a Winesburgian, and that is all I will ever be.

As far as my own supposed unreality is concerned, Bryan Furuness tells me he's not to blame. He says there is another mastermind behind this project, an Indianan who goes by the name "Michael Martone." Bryan tells me that Winesburg, Indiana, is the creation of this Martone guy. What an ego! To take credit for an entire town!

I did some looking around the web for this Martone character. Turns out he doesn't even live in Indiana! I've never left Winesburg! So, I ask, who do you trust to be the real expert on Winesburg? Me, or a guy who lives in a place called "Tuscaloosa"? (I know, it sounds made up.) I wonder how this Martone character would feel if *I* started making up stuff about *him*. Just because he was the first National Guard soldier into Iraq during Operation Desert Storm doesn't make him immune to my imagination. As Ms. Crystal taught us back in junior high, turnabout is fair play.

For now, I'll just say this: If this "Michael Martone" fella ever *does* dare to show his face around these parts, we're going to have some words.

She Drinks Too Much of It

She drinks too much of it, the wine of Winesburg, primarily in the evening when she is too excited to get to sleep or in the afternoon when she tests new batches. She is both producer and consumer of the town's most well-known export. Though of course the town was originally named after the sighs and moans, the complaints and hard-luck stories issuing from the depressives who were first attracted to its flat gray landscape. It mirrored so completely their interior ones, and thus the confusion in the spelling: Winesburg or Whinesburg. As the town folklorist, I prefer the second spelling. It is aspirational. And because she is the keeper of the secret recipes, the princess in the tower, the keeper of the necessary bees, I watch and worry over her. Both the spelling and the mythology of the town depend upon her.

But as I said, she drinks too much of it. How much can the liver take? To be honest, she drinks it from around lunchtime until she falls in bed at night. To be honest, I have never seen her without a glass or jar of it. To be honest, I live next door, and I keep a worried watch over her. I am a bit in love with her, and I can tell you that she lives the life of a nun with the exception of the hour between 2 and 3 AM when she claims she is both fully lucid and god-possessed. He comes every night, she claims. She has never seen him outside of her bedroom, and I have never seen him, not directly, not at all. She is afraid that he might not exist except that he exists so richly for her. Perhaps, it could be argued, she could describe her visitor if she had not had so much to drink. She is aware of this. On the other hand, she is afraid that if she did not drink too much of it he would not come or she would not see him if he did or—the ors are endless. She could row from here to the sun and back with these alternative explanations. She is happy, she says. She loves and she works most bountifully. I am happy for her. She is thirty-five years old and exquisitely beautiful, as was her mother before her, and her grandmother. That is how far back the recipes go in Winesburg.

It has occurred to me, as folklorist, that her mother and grand-mother may have experienced similar nightly visitations when they were producers of the wine, that she herself may be the result of one of those unions. If I am to believe her. And why not? I refuse to believe it is the same god, though that is the way it goes with these myths. Particularly the Greeks, where every sister is married to her brother and every father is also husband to the daughter. The Pantheon is a small town, of course, a bit inbred, like any monarchy.

She always leaves a glass of the nectar by her bed and it is always gone in the morning, so that is proof to her of the visitations. To the atheist, it is proof of too much Ambien. Proof that she drinks too much of it.

You have perhaps driven past the town and seen the winery, which is also her home. It's a small white frame structure located behind the Pentecostal and the Lutheran churches, along the old interurban line.

The house is surrounded by blue and green bottle trees, the names inspired by local flies, but literally consisting of ordinary maples and lindens decorated with empty wine-dark blue and sea-green wine bottles tied by fishing line and hanging from tree limbs, close enough so that the wind makes a bit of a wind chime sound without much breakage. And yes, she knows it is a visual pun, the connecting of fishing line and fly fishing and sea and wine-dark and bottles and wine and whine and wind (which, spelled the same, can still rhyme with wine).

From this you can already tell, or perhaps you knew, that the wine industry in Winesburg is not as it is in other parts of the world. There are no sun-soaked vineyards with globular fruit, no picturesque growers and pickers or stomping and splitting of skin to mix the sugary juice with naturally occurring fruit-skin-dwelling yeasts. There are no wooden vats or more industrial spiraled steel where the fermentation, the must and sweet meet and at times form mead. There are no oak barrels. There is no bottling machine and, except for the purely decorative trees, there are no glass bottles. She uses two-liter plastic bottles from the town recycling. They are quite functional. This is the one variant from the matriarchal line. She sterilizes the bottles before bottling, and there is a satisfying thunking sound as the plastic bottle sucks in on itself during the paradoxical last burst of fermentation, an exhalation of breath that causes the bottle to tighten and pop, like a lid during the canning process.

Of course the part of each batch she drinks herself is fermented and stored in damask glass jelly jars. The wine is sometimes gold and sometimes the odd amber of animal eyes: of dogs, domestic cats, eagles, pigeons, and fish eyes. There is one varietal that is the gray you might get if you mixed the Midwestern/Siberian winter sky and a Shakespearean actress's eyes with water from Lake Erie. It is a favorite with the town's depressives.

The process of making it is quite simple. The sugars are primarily from local flowering weeds, as you might expect. There are other sources of sugar, some quite secret, though some of it is simply her own honey mixed with rainwater. The yeasts are all airborne and hence local. It is thought by some that the most fruitful yeasts originate on her skin. There are plates of mashed flowers and other sweets around her kitchen. When a plate begins to bubble, she knows it's ready. The air is thick with yeast in Winesburg and every home has, at most times, something rising or fermenting either purposefully or otherwise. In fact, fungi in general are plentiful. It is a constant fight to contain them. They spring up under trees, beneath mayapples, they join tentacled hands in solidarity underneath the soil.

One unusual part of the process is the boys who line up at her house at dusk to get the two-liter bottles. There are a dozen or so of these boys. They tie the bottles to the back of their bicycles and they ride on the bumpy abandoned railroad tracks. This is the way meth is made in small towns like Winesburg. But this is not meth she is making. This is ambrosia made from sugars and yeast, from flowering weeds and berries and Shakespeare heroines and out of love and it can only be made in this one place in the universe. It is the one true wine. It appeared once before at the wedding feast at Cana.

And so this is a confession of sorts. I will not say her name, or the location of Winesburg, or any location where you can find the wine or the woman who drinks too much of it. It is our secret. My secret. It is pure and good, and while she sleeps I drink deeply and gratefully from the glass she has left me.

Think what you will. I am a folklorist. I insinuate stories. I import them. I report them. I make them up. It might be said that I drink too much of them. And I am happy here in Winesburg where things have been arranged to work exactly as they are meant to.

Randy Steeple

All sorts come to tell their stories. Grudge Wright makes bad jokes about his bad jokes, safe here from heckler-thrown tomatoes. Reverend Dave recounts the day he saved Pastor John from strychnine poisoning, thanks to the Lord's divine intervention, of course. Countless citizens come with conspiracy theories and claims of abduction, waving blurry photos of UFOs, swearing the device in their hands, though it looks like an eggbeater, is actually an alien probe. Sometimes I feel like the personal psychiatrist for the whole town, but no one comes here to lie on a red couch and work out their problems. No one comes to talk to me.

They often forget I'm here, behind the TK-780, a dinosaur of a camera, a relic from broadcast past. I operate the lights and the soundboard, too, and I sweep up the studio when we aren't live. I pretty much run the place now—after the programming director, Mr. Diamond, died and the station switched to cable, no one else saw the point in continuing. One person could operate the station just fine, and that person ended up being me. This wasn't how I'd planned my life. Margot and I were supposed to get out of here together. I'd dreamt of Tinseltown when I was a kid, but after all my applications to film schools were answered with regretful rejection letters, I got the cameraman job here, at Winesburg Public Access Television, WEEP-TV.

The station is housed in a little building out on the outskirts of town, the transmission tower right behind it, concealed in an old grain elevator. When I started, we had a whole crew working lights and sound and editing, even though our programming was mostly tapes of church sermons and community theater, old home movies thought valuable only by the people in them, or the people not quite in them, the hands guiding each home video camera's Cyclops eye, showing us what they saw in the Little League pop flies and amusement park vacations. Mr. Diamond liked to make sure there was programming around the clock, so we scheduled interviews with citizens, filmed documentaries about Winesburg. We aired them late at night or on holidays, those rare moments when no one else had a show they wanted us to show.

I asked him once why he bothered to do this, why give himself—and us—more work. He was always chewing on a cigar, speaking out of the side of his mouth, but he took it out when he answered me. He said, "People in Winesburg are constantly looking elsewhere, out into the world, saying nothing happens here." Nothing happens here. That was something Margot had always said, something she wrote in her letters to me. "But things do happen here," Mr. Diamond said. "They happen all the time." He said it was up to us to show them, to provide the proof.

Margot kept asking when I was going to meet her out in LA, where she was singing old soul tunes in bars. She said a record executive had given her his card after a performance, that she was waiting on him to return her call. I told her I was saving up the money and then I would pack up and join her. For a while that was true. When it wasn't anymore, it was because I couldn't abandon Mr. Diamond. I didn't want to let him down. I wanted to see what he saw in Winesburg. I wasn't going to leave until I saw something happen, something I could tell Margot, a story I could tell people elsewhere when they asked where, exactly, I was from.

Back then, everybody in town still watched WEEP-TV. This was partly in hopes of seeing someone they knew up on screen, to feel like secondhand celebrities. Mostly, though, it was out of necessity: there were only twelve channels on the dial. It was a canal of channels, a channel, a main stream mainstream. Today, there are thousands, gulfs of them, seas. We don't see the same seas, aren't caught in the same currents anymore. Sure, the public still uses the public access studio, but nobody watches what anyone else airs: the lonely librarian, acting out scenes from *Little Women*, urging someone, anyone, to pull that book from the shelf; the man who has personally handled all the job outsourcing in our town, now trying to outsource his own job; the schoolchildren with their hands mittened in multicolored socks, button eyes, and felt mouths, their nonsensical puppet shows that always end with a shark-finned sock appearing and tearing through the other socks, ripping their sock-skin away and leaving their handlike skeletons exposed and human and wanting not to speak but to be held.

Some of the younger kids don't understand how live television works, and they rush home after their broadcast, hoping to beat themselves there, turning on the television and looking for their own eyes looking out at them, the afterimage of their image, after.

Friends and parents and grandparents and sons and daughters and coworkers and ex-lovers and fathers-in-law and brides-to-be all make promises to watch the shows of their loved ones when they air, but no one ever finds the channel on time, they always just miss it. Or maybe they forget. Or maybe they can't find the remote. Or maybe they're busy. Or maybe something better is on: the big game that's a tie in the fourth quarter, the six o'clock news, the talk show host saying stay tuned we're coming right back after these messages, music videos on one of the channels that still play them, the sitcom with the theme song everyone knows all the words to tonight at eight-seven-central, the nine o'clock news, the series premieres, the season finales, the biopics and reality shows, the cartoons and standup comedy specials and on and on and on until someone turns it off.

Margot's letters to me had long since stopped when Mr. Diamond jumped from the top of the grain elevator. He left me a tape, with instructions to air it on WEEP-TV daily. But the tape didn't have anything on it. Frame after frame of black blank nothingness. I don't know what he meant to record on it, if he'd meant to record anything at all, what it would mean if he hadn't. Sometimes, though, I air a couple minutes of the tape, maybe an hour, just to see if anyone will call, will ask to speak with the manager, will tell me the station is off the air.

And sometimes, late at night, I air the old Super 8 films I made as a teenager, the ones that failed to get me out of this town where I used to think nothing happened: the campy sci-fi epic about alien bootleggers during Prohibition; the heist movie where one actor plays all the characters doing the heisting, as well as the prized object being heisted; the romance that failed because she left and he stayed and that's just how it was, how it had to be.

And some of those sometime sometimes, I turn the camera on and stand in front of it. I look up at the blinking lit-up letters spelling ON AIR in the air. I imagine the bubble-round coelacanth eye of the TK-780 lens drip-dropping this little drop deep into the great widescreen digital sea of static snow and scenes unseen. But maybe there's someone sitting at home, unable to sleep, unable to find anything but infomercials and scrambled smut and a listing list listing what's on the other channels. And then, there: a man, me, staring out from the screen, unmoving and silent. The person sitting at home, the audience, my audience, leans close to the television set, watching, anxious to see what I'll do.

Look. I am opening my mouth. Tonight's big show is beginning to begin. Don't go anywhere. Don't touch that dial. Something is about to happen.

Acknowledgments by
Marny Vanderroost

1 box spiral noodles, cooked
2 cans cream of mushroom soup
1 lb. ground beef, browned
½ lb. bacon, cooked and chopped
1 large onion, minced
2 stalks celery, chopped
1 box Velveeta
potato chips, crushed
salt and pepper to taste

What you hold in your hands is the work of many fine people, the pieces of their lives pulled together to form the picture of a town. It seems to me like one of my casseroles. I started to write out the cooking instructions in detail but it hardly seemed necessary. Everyone knows how to make a casserole: you mix the ingredients—even those that don't seem so savory alone—and let the heat transform them into something that will feed everyone.

Here in Winesburg, that heat is contact and closeness, conflict and cooperation. We move in a flow of people who've known us most of our lives: bumping elbows, using first names, nicknames, cuss words as names, the wrong name misheard twenty years ago that was adopted out of politeness. Heat also comes from possibility, and possibilities passed by. Everyone has regrets: a lost invitation to a dance, or being too shy, too poor, too embarrassed to ask in the first place. Life goes on and you grow up and marry and have babies, and it's good and quiet and normal, but you wonder: what if? In a place like Winesburg your What If likely lives within a stone's throw, two lanes over with his wife Jane who has that smile like a paring knife. Your What If walks his yellow retriever past your house every day.

The first person to thank for this book is Ernest Fassber, mayor of our town, and the hot, creamy soup that binds us together. For this project he cleared away so much red tape. I love him to death. I could wrap myself around him and simply melt. Together we'd make some new world you'd never expect from a can and a box you got at the IGA.

The citizens and visitors have been so giving with their time, open with their secrets: Mr. Derrida (who offered to review my personal hierarchy), that quiet librarian girl we all think will snap one day, Grudge Wright and the others. Even that odd little Inspector man. Especially him, I suppose. Some towns keep their crazy hidden, but we scatter it on top like potato chips.

I would like to thank the spiritual leaders of Winesburg: the priests, that funny little rabbi, the bartenders and janitors and the homeless man who sings the blues like a suicidal angel and even the divorced Unitarian girl with the short hair. We acknowledge the men who work, the women who work harder, crying children, the grain elevator dominating the skyline, wet parking lots, the empty bandshell, and the sad ambition of the Community Players. We acknowledge closed doors and a gap in the curtains for the Neighborhood Watch, and the retired people of Winesburg—the farmer brothers Leon and Marshall Harnes in their wind-warped wooden house, Jack Ballentine who could shape any metal part from raw stock—whose collective knowledge of growing, making, building, living quietly, is washing away in increments each year with the topsoil.

We live on land so flat you can see the curvature of the earth at the horizon. We acknowledge that we walk on the skin of northern states scraped clean by glaciers that deposited the fertile soil here in Winesburg. Liz Heckathorn, the gravedigger, calls out the layers of limestone, sandstone, dolostone, siltstone, shale, mudstone, and flashes of gypsum as she digs down to lay another Winesburg generation in place.

We acknowledge that our town is small. We acknowledge that Indiana is not enough for some.

You are holding this book at the best moment. The casserole is complete, out of the oven, resting on the stove. The guests have arrived and are waiting at the table. Before I dish up the plates alone in the kitchen, I sink both hands into that perfect hot goodness. It burns, almost, and on that line of pain and love I say a prayer for all of those about to be fed.

Credits

Some of these stories have appeared in *Booth* magazine.

Contributors

BARBARA BEAN
"Frances Parker"

Barbara Bean is the author of *Dream House,* a collection of stories. Her fiction has appeared in the *Georgia Review,* the *Colorado Review,* the *North American Review,* and the *Northwest Review,* among others. She lives in Greencastle, Indiana, where she taught creative writing and literature at DePauw University.

Queen Anne's lace, horsemint, butterfly weed, the great blue heron, and buzzards, always buzzards—July in Indiana.

KATE BERNHEIMER
"Professor Helen C. Andersen"

Kate Bernheimer is the author of a novel trilogy and the story collections *Horse, Flower, Bird* and *How a Mother Weaned Her Girl from Fairy Tales,* and the editor of four anthologies, including the World Fantasy Award–winning and best-selling *My Mother She Killed Me, My Father He Ate Me: Forty New Fairy Tales* and *xo Orpheus: Fifty New Myths.*

ROBIN BLACK
"Beau Morrow"

Robin Black, author of the books *If I Loved You I Would Tell You This* and *Life Drawing*, is one of those irritating East Coasters who had never heard of Indiana until she was nineteen, driving cross-country with three women, when there was a stop in Indianapolis, a parking lot at night, strangely bright lights everywhere, someone needing a cup of coffee; but Black didn't leave the car, so technically she has never set foot in the state. She hopes to remedy that one day. She hears it's nice.

KAREN BRENNAN
"Pete, Waste Lab Technician"

Karen Brennan is the author of seven books of varying genres, including fiction, nonfiction, and poetry. She is a core faculty member of the Warren Wilson College MFA Program for Writers and a Professor Emerita at the University of Utah. Karen Brennan has never been to Indiana and has acquired most of her knowledge of that state from the plume facile of Michael Martone. Her boyfriend Stephen reports that while driving across the country in 1967, his car broke down in Indiana due to a faulty valve. The Indiana mechanic removed the valve and, for the rest of the cross-country drive, his car—a "clunker" anyway—sounded like a machine gun.

BRIAN BUCKBEE
"Clyde"

Brian Buckbee grew up in Illinois not far from the western border of Indiana, went to school in Ohio not far from the eastern border of Indiana, failed to marry a woman he loved from central Indiana, and raced into and out of Indiana fast as he could up Route 65 one terrifying night during the tornado outbreak of June 1990. For a short time he worked as the head security guard at the Field of Light Bulbs in Pulaski County. On November 1, 1987, Brian made a pilgrimage to the Hoosier Dome to see a U2 concert, and was rewarded—and altered forever—by a surprise performance by the rarely seen Dalton Brothers, who themselves call into question what is real, what is not, and surely inspired Brian to write about Clyde, Vice President Hendricks, Leonard Nimoy, and the famously elusive NBA star Billy Joe Cuthbert.

SHANNON CAIN
"Occupy Winesburg"

Last year, Shannon Cain drove across the United States on the interstates and didn't even realize she'd been through Indiana until she reached Virginia and consulted a map. Reeling from that loss, she now sticks to the back roads. Her first book, *The Necessity of Certain Behaviors,* won the Drue Heinz Literature Prize. Her stories have also been recognized with the O. Henry Prize, two Pushcarts, and a grant from the NEA. Shannon makes a living as a manuscript consultant and writing coach. She lives in Paris, France.

SHERRIE FLICK
"Emmalene's Bakery and Bait Shop"

Sherrie Flick is the author of the novel *Reconsidering Happiness* and the forthcoming short story collection *Whiskey, Etc.* Her flash fiction appears in many anthologies and journals, including *Flash*

Fiction Forward and *New Sudden Fiction*. She lives in Pittsburgh but dreams of Winesburg, Indiana, as the heart of the heart of the Midwest. Her website is sherrieflick.com.

BRYAN FURUNESS
Co-editor

Bryan Furuness was born in East Chicago, Indiana, a town whose identity crisis is apparent in its name. Is it Chicago or is it Indiana? He grew up on Chicago time watching the Chicago Bears play on Chicago television stations. At the same time, the town is clearly located in Indiana, a state which Bryan knew a great deal about thanks largely to his mother, who taught state history to her fourth graders and took Bryan along on all her trips to state parks and historical sites. So the answer is: Yes and yes. But also: No and no. No one from Chicago has ever counted East Chicago as Actual Chicago. And the rest of Indiana openly despises and disavows this strip of industrialized Indiana along the lake—referred to as "da region"—because of the unions, and left-leaning politics, and general lack of corn. (Another possible answer, given by a coast-dweller, would be: Who cares? You're all Midwesterners.) Eventually, Bryan would drift downstate to Indianapolis, though he set his novel, *The Lost Episodes of Revie Bryson,* in the no-man's-land of the region. Now he teaches at Butler University, where he also serves as the advisor for *Manuscripts,* the undergraduate literary magazine. Next to his desk is a bookshelf containing a copy of every issue of *Manuscripts* dating back to 1934, including a few issues filled with stories by a young Michael Martone. Now he thinks the answer is yes and no and yes and no—the region like a steel ball held in perfect tension between two magnets with like poles.

ROXANE GAY
"Tara Jenkins"

Roxane Gay lives and writes in the Midwest. She recently moved to Indiana to teach at Purdue University.

B. J. HOLLARS
"Reverend Dave"

B. J. Hollars is the author of three books of nonfiction—most recently *Dispatches from the Drownings*—as well as a collection of stories, *Sightings*. A native of Fort Wayne, Indiana (where a bust of Michael Martone is displayed prominently in the entryway of the public library), Hollars currently serves as an Assistant Professor of Creative Writing at the University of Wisconsin-Eau Claire.

C. J. HRIBAL
"Jackie Patch" and "Julie Patch"

C. J. Hribal is the author of the novels *The Company Car* and *American Beauty* and the short fiction collections *Matty's Heart* and *The Clouds in Memphis*, which won the AWP Award for Short Fiction. He also edited *The Boundaries of Twilight: Czecho-Slovak Writing from the New World*. He is the Louise Edna Goeden Professor of English at Marquette University, and a member of the fiction faculty at the Warren Wilson College MFA Program for Writers. He fondly remembers putting pennies on the railroad tracks in West Lafayette, Indiana, with his children, and hiking along the Wabash River with his friends. He also once helped paint a house in Vevay, Indiana, for his brother-in-law, and likes that some of the rest areas on Indiana's toll roads are named after Indiana writers, though the idea of privatizing the rest stops was just plain silly.

ANDREW HUDGINS
"Raymond Snow"

Andrew Hudgins is the author, most recently, of a book of poems, *A Clown at Midnight,* and a memoir about being a compulsive joke-teller, *The Joker.* He teaches at The Ohio State University, and is married to the novelist Erin McGraw, a graduate of the MFA Program at Indiana University. He spent many happy hours in and around Bloomington when he was first seeing her and she was teaching at DePauw.

SEAN LOVELACE
"The Processed Cheese Product Man"

Sean Lovelace lives in Indiana, near a variety of corn, where he directs the Creative Writing Program at Ball State University. His latest collection is about Velveeta. He blogs at seanlovelace.com. He likes to run, far.

LEE MARTIN
"Miss Gladys"

Lee Martin has published three memoirs, most recently *Such a Life.* He is also the author of four novels, including *Break the Skin* and *The Bright Forever,* a finalist for the 2006 Pulitzer Prize in Fiction. He grew up in Illinois just across the river from Vincennes, Indiana, the land of George Rogers Clark, *Alice of Old Vincennes,* Red Skelton, and peach orchards and melon patches. He now lives in Columbus, Ohio, and teaches in the MFA Program at The Ohio State University.

"Biddlebaum Cowley Reefy & Swift LLP," "City Manager,"
"Amanda Patch," "Dale Rumsey," "Ken of Ottumwa,"
"Jacques Derrida Writes Postcards to Himself from a
Diner in Winesburg, Indiana," "Constance H. Wootin,"
"Walt 'Helper' Voltz," "Found in the *Placebo:* The Yearbook
of Emile Durkheim High School," "Gregg Pitman," "Carol
Clay," "The Cantor Quadruplets," and "Inspector 4"

Michael Martone was born in Fort Wayne, Indiana. Growing up
in Indiana, a teenaged Martone, along with many of his age-mates,
took summertime employment in the agricultural sector of the
state's economy. It was a rite of passage to ride the mechanical
carriers through the extensive seed corn fields that surrounded the
nearby small town of Winesburg, Indiana, detasseling the plant in
order to produce hybridized strains of the grain. Martone enjoyed
drifting above the tasseling plants, the ocean of vinyl green corn,
a vortex swirling around him. He usually worked in fields planted
in 4:1 panels, four female rows of one variety to be detasseled and
one bull row left to pollinate. The blocks created a wavy pattern
in the fields he sailed over, carefully unspooling the threads of the
tassels from the tangle of leaves the machines had missed. At other
times he rouged as well, walking the shaded rows searching for
the volunteer starts and preventing their undesirable pollen from
taking root in the precious hybridizing. At night, after the long day
of gleaning every strand from every plant, Martone would dream
he was a dusty bee or a caked butterfly, staggering from one forest
of tassels to the next into the chromatic confusion of the morning. And in the fall, after school had started up again, he returned
to the now harvested fields, the sharp stubble laced with frost,

and huddled under the scratchy wool blankets in the back of an old buckboard bumping through the empty fields near the small town of Winesburg, a passenger on one of the last real hayrides in Indiana, and whispered to the girl beside him the intricate secrets of the intriguing sex life of corn.

SAM MARTONE
"Randy Steeple"

Sam Martone lives and writes in Tempe, Arizona. Growing up, he celebrated Christmas with his grandparents, who set up hundreds of animatronic singing and dancing Santa Clauses throughout their house in Fort Wayne, Indiana. Every year, when Sam Martone arrived, his grandparents took him through the house, showing off the new additions, pressing buttons and motioning in front of sensors, saying, "Take a look at this one. This one here."

ERIN MCGRAW
"Deanne Stovers"

Erin McGraw is the author of six books of fiction: three novels and three collections of stories. She lived in Indiana for ten years, first writing and then teaching, and bears the Hoosier mark. To this day she is convinced that she can't buy liquor on Sundays.

JOYELLE MCSWEENEY
"The Bottle"

An invasive species with lustrous petals and a glabrous stem, non-native Joyelle McSweeney teaches at the University of Notre Dame and lives in South Bend. She is the author of six books of poetry and prose, most recently *Percussion Grenade* and *Salamandrine, 8 Gothics*. Her play *Dead Youth, or, the Leaks* won the inaugural

Leslie Scalapino Prize for Innovative Women Playwrights. A book of critical essays, *The Necropastoral: Poetry, Media, Occults,* was published in 2014. McSweeney credits life in South Bend and Mishawaka for the development of her theory of the necropastoral, a gothic ecopoetics based on decay and uncanny effervescence. Her book *Salamandrine* takes Michiana as its muse, and her work *Dead Youth* was inspired both by Melville's *Benito Cereno* and by learning that the teenage Somali "pirate" Abduwali Muse is incarcerated in Terre Haute. She and Indiana have a co-parasitic relationship of imbrication, exultation, and mistrust.

VALERIE MINER
"Triple Crown"

Valerie Miner is the author of fourteen books, including novels, story collections, and a memoir. Her newest novel is *Traveling with Spirits.* Her work has appeared in the *Village Voice, Salmagundi, Ploughshares, Triquarterly,* the *Georgia Review, Prairie Schooner,* the *Gettysburg Review,* and elsewhere. She is a professor and artist in residence at Stanford University. Her website is valerieminer. com. Some of her best friends are from Indiana.

SUSAN NEVILLE
"She Drinks Too Much of It"

Susan Neville lives on the northeast corner of the double circle that is at the center (capital?) of Winesburg. To picture this double circle, picture the moon eclipsing the sun, or picture a Life Saver, or picture an eye. She lives either in the northeast corner of the moon or the northeast corner of the hole within the candy or the northeast corner of the pupil of a person lying down with his or her head to the north, depending on what you are picturing. She has lived here (or there, depending again on your point of view) her whole life. From this (or that) place she has written several books and flung them out into the world. She has also raised two children and taught many many students who have flung themselves out into that same world, the one outside of the double circle.

KELCEY ERVICK PARKER
"Limberlost"

Kelcey Ervick Parker is the author of *Liliane's Balcony,* set at Frank Lloyd Wright's Fallingwater, and the story collection *For Sale by Owner.* She directs the Creative Writing Program at Indiana University South Bend, which is just a couple of hours from Limberlost Swamp, setting of Gene Stratton-Porter's novel *A Girl of the Limberlost.* Although she is not from Indiana originally, she could probably say, as her narrator does, "I'm from here now."

EDWARD PORTER
"Howard Garfield, Balladeer"

Edward Porter's short fiction has appeared in the *Hudson Review,* the *Gettysburg Review, Colorado Review, Barrelhouse, Booth, Best New American Voices,* and elsewhere. He has been a Madison Fellow, a MacDowell Fellow, and a teaching fellow at Millsaps College, and is currently a Stegner Fellow at Stanford University. In a former life as a touring actor, he crisscrossed the Midwest and spent many a golden evening drinking and swapping tales in Don Hall's Guesthouse in Fort Wayne, Indiana.

ETHEL ROHAN
"Dark Stars"

Ethel Rohan published her latest work in *The Lineup: 25 Provocative Women Writers* (2015); *Drivel: Deliciously Bad Writing by Your Favorite Authors* (2014); and *Flash Fiction International* (2015). The peony, Indiana's state flower, is a favorite. Rohan is also ridiculously partial to wine. To find out more, visit ethelrohan.com.

VALERIE SAYERS
"Cleaning Lady to the Stars"

Valerie Sayers, Professor of English at the University of Notre Dame, has lived in Indiana since 1993, a fact endlessly fascinating to her old friends in Brooklyn. She is the author of six novels as well as many stories, essays, and reviews.

GREG SCHWIPPS
"Burt Coble, Catman"

Greg Schwipps was born and raised on a working farm in Milan, Indiana. He co-authored *Fishing for Dummies, 2nd Edition,* and his first novel, *What This River Keeps,* was reissued by Indiana University Press in 2012. In 2010 he won the Eugene & Marilyn Glick Indiana Authors Award in the Emerging Writer category. Greg is currently an Associate Professor of English at DePauw University. He and his wife Alissa live with their two sons, Milan and Arlo, in Wilbur, Indiana.

"'Manchild' Morrison: The Best That Almost Was"

Porter Shreve is the author of four novels. His latest, *The End of the Book* (2014), is partly inspired by Sherwood Anderson's *Winesburg, Ohio* and takes place in both present-day and turn-of-the-century Chicago. Shreve directed the MFA Program at Purdue University in West Lafayette, Indiana, for eight years. He now teaches in the low-residency MFA Program at Ashland University in Ohio and in the MFA Program at the University of San Francisco.

GEORGE SINGLETON
"Grudge Wright"

George Singleton is the author of six collections of stories, two novels, and a book of writing advice. He holds the John C. Cobb Chair in the Humanities at Wofford College in Spartanburg, South Carolina.

DEB OLIN UNFERTH
"Dear Class of 2011"

Deb Olin Unferth is the author, most recently, of the memoir *Revolution,* finalist for the National Book Critics Circle Award and a *New York Times* Editors' Choice. Her work has appeared in *Harper's,* the *New York Times, McSweeney's,* the *Boston Review,* the *Believer, Conjunctions,* and elsewhere. She has received three Pushcart Prizes and a Creative Capital Grant for Innovative Literature. She grew up in Chicago and spent her childhood running up and down the Indiana sand dunes.

JIM WALKE
"Acknowledgments by Marny Vanderroost"

Jim Walke helps the Bioinformatics Institute at Virginia Tech write very large biomedical research grant proposals. The rest of the time he works on a novel, hikes with Rudyard Kipling—his dog of dubious intelligence—and watches hockey. His work has appeared in several journals and anthologies, including most recently the *Massachusetts Review* and *Home of the Brave: Somewhere in the Sand.* On long drives to the South, Jim splits Indiana lengthwise on state highways and back roads rather than the soulless expressway.

Regardless of rivers crossed and boundaries on a map, he always knows he has reached Indiana when a gas station attendant or passerby makes a smartass cutting remark in the nicest possible manner.

CLAIRE VAYE WATKINS
"Mari, Waiting"

Claire Vaye Watkins, a 2014 Guggenheim Fellow, is the author of the story collection *Battleborn,* which won the Story Prize, the Dylan Thomas Prize, the New York Public Library Young Lions Fiction Award, the Rosenthal Family Foundation Award from the American Academy of Arts and Letters, and a Silver Pen Award from the Nevada Writers Hall of Fame. As a girl she spent a summer in the rivers and swimming holes near Elkhart, and has often returned to the Indiana of her imagination since.

Book Club Guide

Prepared by Amanda Patch with the aid of the Ladies of the Ladies Book Clubs of Our Lady of the Circumcision, Roman Catholic Church, and the Greek Orthodox Church of Saint Dymphna located in Winesburg, Indiana

This reading group guide for the book *Winesburg, Indiana* includes an introduction and questions for discussion with suggestions for enhancing your book club's group reading of the book *Winesburg, Indiana*. The following questions (we hope) will help your reading group discover new angles and interesting topics as you grope with the discussable aspects of this book. We pray that these ideas (more like asides, really, or hastily recorded spontaneous utterances or Freudian slips or [at the very least] exasperated extemporaneous train wrecks of thought) we gleaned from our own ongoing and (it seems) endless contestations with this book, *Winesburg, Indiana* (which presents itself as an innocent collection of transcriptions of our own [the citizens of the said town of Winesburg, Indiana] dark musings, desperate confessions, miscalculated memoirs, autocorrected autobiographies, therapeutic narratives, deranged screeds, uncorroborated gossip, dangerously personal digressions, and befuddled baffled protestations of personal history) will enrich your conversation and increase your enjoyment of the book, the aforementioned *Winesburg, Indiana* and (it seems) the overly chatty and personal boundary-crossing citizenry of the eponymous municipality of Winesburg, Indiana, our home town.

INTRODUCTION

Published in 2015, *Winesburg, Indiana* is a modern classic that documents the inner lives of the inhabitants of a typical small Midwestern town in a series of narratives that originally wished to employ "free indirect discourse" but quickly settled into distracted and meandering digressions of its characters' individual neuroses, psychological dysfunctions, and generally deranged psychopathies that created a somewhat sad but also a euphoric survivor-like guilt-free guilt in the reader as he or she negotiates a post-post-traumatic landscape peopled by anxious people anxious to get all the anxiety out.

TOPICS AND QUESTIONS FOR DISCUSSION

1. **Discuss the anthology format of the book. Why can't there just be one author of this book instead of a whole bunch of authors who all appear to have something different in mind?** The books *Winesburg, Ohio* and *Spoon River Anthology* both have just one author, and they seem to have kept it all together. It worked out just fine (in Dorcus Henry's opinion in any case). **And while we are on the subject, why did we have to have a book at all about us and our town of Winesburg when that other book about the other Winesburg already**

existed? If you ask us (and you can't since we have been instructed by the City Manager not to discuss the book openly but add our furtive meetings on the topic to the litany of secrets already catalogued and presented here in the book we are talking about not talking about) it seems like a pervasive and pernicious failure of the imagination.

2. **Who did you identify with the most? Did you see parts of yourself in any one specific character?** You might gather this is a big problem with us as many of us find ourselves as characters in the book *Winesburg, Indiana* and in the town Winesburg, Indiana and upon finding ourselves there or there, we go on to find we really don't know who we really are. What is perhaps more disturbing is that if you ask any one of us (and remember, you really shouldn't) we would probably say that we identified more closely with somebody other than our own selves rendered in these pages, estranged and alienated as we are from ourselves' selves. This is a real problem for the Cantor Quadruplets who beyond suffering the garden-variety abandonment issues are multiply afflicted by a highly amplified separation anxiety making it impossible for any one quad to differentiate one quad from another and all of them reflected again and again in the mirrored finish of that Airstream Trailer of theirs.

3. **Choose one character from the book and discuss if he or she is sympathetic. Could you imagine being friends with him or her? Why or why not?** Really, we would like to know. We would like to be liked. It is difficult for us just to sustain a book club or two in this village as the Reading Group Guides

we utilize at the back of the books we read rarely prompt any discussion really. We tend not to like each other, as our ability to like ourselves is problematic. Most of us believe that as we read the books silently and alone, our meetings should be conducted mostly in silence and its members distributed evenly throughout the rooms of that month's host's house. I suspect that the meetings of my group most often meet at my house because my house has many rooms and many closets in its many rooms. What discussion there is is most often muffled, baffled as we are by the books, the architecture of the house, and each other.

4. **Who is Emile Durkheim?** No, really, we would like to know this too. **And why is our high school named after him?** And why were the lockers at the high school locked by overly complicated combination locks that seemed to also randomly and without warning or explanation recalibrate the combinations of a number of lockers each and every morning so that the halls, even after the last bell before homeroom, were filled with students entering, again and again, obsolete formulas on the locker's dial, punctuated by protracted bouts of staring off into space, displaying an aspect that could only be characterized as profound forgetfulness and/or ordinary substantial and persistent dread?

5. Henry David Thoreau wrote in *Walden,* "The mass of men lead lives of quiet desperation. What is called resignation is confirmed desperation. From the desperate city you go into the desperate country, and have to console yourself with the bravery of minks and muskrats. A stereotyped but unconscious

despair is concealed even under what are called the games and amusements of mankind. There is no play in them, for this comes after work. But it is a characteristic of wisdom not to do desperate things." **Does this sound like anyone you know from the book?** We named our grand park after the Sage of Walden who, we understand, still had his mother do his laundry even after he removed to his cabin in the woods. Many of us read *Winesburg, Indiana* while in hammocks we installed among the trees of Throw Park (a misspelling on the original plat map that seems to have stuck around). There are plenty of muskrats and minks there as well, inhabiting the banks and mudflats of the West Fork of the Fork River, a disappearing river, alas, in this underlying karst region.

6. *Winesburg, Indiana* grapples with complex, universally difficult stages of birth, life, and death. **What reflections, if any, did it inspire in you about your own life? Whose life story resonated most deeply in you?** You don't really have to answer that. Having gotten to know us by reading our various and vexed life stories, allow us to say it may just have been enough for you to observe from afar (watching each episode unfold and the whole crazed catastrophe of this place) with pity and horror in order to exorcise and exercise your own cathartic apparatus of feeling, a sump pump if you will, for the flush of synthetic and synaptic emotional neap tides.

CPSIA information can be obtained at www.ICGtesting.com
Printed in the USA
LVOW10s1502170715

446649LV00005B/503/P

9 780253 016881